Ordinary Perils

Stories

Ordinary Perils

Stories by

Ann Robinson

Peter E. Randall Publisher
Portsmouth, New Hampshire
2002

Peter E. Randall Publisher
Box 4726, Portsmouth, NH 03802
www.PERPublisher.com

Distributed by University Press of New England
Hanover and London
First Edition February 2003.

Cover art: "Bloom Beneath the Snow," 2001, by Louise Link Rath
Cover design by Grace Peirce
Back cover photograph by Al Karevy
Book design by Deidre Randall

Library of Congress Cataloging-in-Publication Data

Robinson, Ann, 1937-
Ordinary perils : stories / by Ann Robinson.
p. cm.
ISBN 1-931807-09-4 (alk. paper)
1. United States--Social life and customs--Fiction. 2. Middle age--Fiction. I. Title.
PS3618.O318 O73 2002
813'.6--dc21

2002013227

The following stories have appeared previously in print: "The Elf Gig": *Yankee*, December 1984; "Saving a Life": *The Monadnock Reader*, 1990; "The Pretender": *Oxford Magazine*, Fall/Winter 1992; "Near Moon": *The Nightshade Nightstand Reader*, 1995; "Sanctuary": *Ellipsis: Literature and Art*, Spring 1999.

Anton Chekhov quoted in A. Skaftymov's article "Principles of Structure in Chekhov's Plays" reprinted in *Chekhov, A Collection of Critical Essays*, Robert Louis Jackson, ed. Englewood Cliffs, NJ: Prentice Hall, 1967.

But really, in life people are not every minute shooting each other, hanging themselves, and making declarations of love. And they are not saying clever things every minute. For the most part, they eat, drink, hang about, and talk nonsense . . . Let everything on stage be just as complex and at the same time just as simple as in life. People dine, merely dine, but at that moment their happiness is being made or their life is being smashed.

—Anton Chekhov

This book is for my husband, Jim, and for our three daughters, Nancy, Maggie, and Jeanne, who now have children of their own.

Contents

THE PRETENDER

She'd often dreamed of what it might feel like to bathe and dress such a child, to shampoo his hair and fold his clothing. As she followed him into the shower cubicle and watched him pull down his trunks, she noticed his tan marks from the summer before. He stood in the shower stall with his back toward her. It was all she could do to keep from touching those small, perfectly formed shoulder blades, those beautifully molded buttocks. *This could be the body of my child,* she thought as she turned on the water and adjusted the temperature.

Later, when they were in her car heading north, she told herself that she first thought of taking him away with her then. But if she were to be completely honest with herself, she would have to admit that it had started with the other secretaries daring her to use the spa at the convention center. The attendant who handed her a folded towel containing ice cubes and told her to breathe into it shut the dungeonlike door and disappeared, leaving her alone in the steam room. Soon she felt faint from the excessive heat. Something about the place reminded her of an operating room that, though cold and light by contrast, had produced a similar sensation. When they'd put her to sleep it was as though a door slammed inside her head, but she remembered that a nurse in the recovery room had said she was sorry about the loss of the baby.

After the steam bath, she walked through the convention center's ornate lobby, where secretaries, dressed for cocktails, were gathered in clumps like brilliantly colored irises. In the shopping arcade she paused to look in the window of an infants clothing boutique. Pastel-hued stretch suits were spread-eagled against the walls, and shoppers pushed strollers stuffed with chubby babies between the racks of lilliputian garments. The babies' drowsy countenances told her it was nap time. They made her think of her own lost child.

The next morning, she went for an early swim at the indoor pool, which had been decorated to look like a greenhouse, with giant murals depicting tropical flowers of every description. For the moment the area was deserted, but as she stood there, a woman came out of the dressing rooms with a little boy. They walked to the edge of the pool. The woman was pretty—tall and slim, with shoulder-length dark hair pulled back into a bun—and she wore a slightly constructed one-piece suit of vivid red that matched the hibiscus blossoms in the mural. The boy was small and wiry, and he bounced with excitement as they approached the water. He wore Hawaiian-print boxers—miniatures, she imagined, of his father's trunks. She guessed his age at four, the age of her nephew, and the age her son would have been, had he lived. They entered the water. In his eagerness the boy slipped, and his head went beneath the surface. She was startled until she saw that his mother had kept hold of his hand and could pull him to a standing position. He might have been frightened, but instead he laughed. "The water tickles my nose," he said, and when she heard the sound of his laughter, she was enchanted.

She watched the boy push away from the woman and begin to swim. "That's excellent, Paul!" the woman said, clapping her hands in delight. "You've remembered everything! Now come back here while *I* take a swim." He obeyed immediately, and sat on the steps while his mother swam slowly to the opposite end of the pool, setting the water in motion with her easy strokes.

What a perfect life they must lead, she thought. She had decided they were mother and child, wealthy, able to stay in the finest hotels. She envied them their freedom to choose any pleasures they desired.

The boy saw her and waved, and she waved back. She stepped out of her sweatpants and walked to the steps where he sat waiting for his mother to finish her laps. "I'm not supposed to swim until Mommy gets back here," he said, "although I can swim perfectly well."

"I can see that," she said. "Is the water warm?"

"*I* think so."

She stuck her toes in. "Ooh. Not as warm as I expected."

"But warmer than the ocean in Maine."

"Oh, much," she agreed, though she'd never been there.

"Let me see you swim."

"I'm not very good."

"How do you know?"

"Someone told me once." Feeling self-conscious, she walked deeper into the water and began to swim clumsily away from the boy. Soon she was breathless from the unaccustomed exertion, and had to hang onto the gutter to rest. She watched the woman swim gracefully back and forth and marveled at her stamina.

The boy was getting restless. "Enough!" he yelled. "It's my turn, Mommy!"

"Just a paddle, because it's almost time for my massage. You'll have to sit up there while I'm gone," she said, pointing to the deck chairs. "You can wrap up in one of those nice big towels and stay warm till I get back."

"No!" he shouted. "I'm not getting out! You promised me a long swim." He started to cry.

"Excuse me for eavesdropping, but I'd be glad to keep an eye on him while you're gone. We can stay here, in the shallow water," she offered, indicating the area cordoned off with yellow rope. "Really. You wouldn't have to worry."

The woman hesitated.

"I'm—a nurse."

The woman smiled. "In that case, well, it's very kind of you, Miss . . ."

"Johnson. Terry Johnson." The name came to her easily, though she had never lied about her identity before.

She hadn't wanted to give him the sleeping pill, but Paul started to become frightened. It wasn't even hers. It was her roommate's; she'd taken the small bottle of Dalmane from the girl's cosmetic bag while she was in the lobby buying souvenirs. In the McDonald's where they stopped for lunch she gave him the pill, which she halved first, saying it was easier to swallow that way.

"What is this?" Paul asked.

"Aspirin. You said you were chilly after your shower, and this will keep you from getting a cold."

"I don't take aspirin. I take Tylenol."

"Did I say aspirin? I meant Tylenol. Anyway, they're the same."

"No, they're not."

She took a deep breath. "All right," she said, trying to keep from sounding annoyed. "They're not. But this is Tylenol, and you need to take it."

"It doesn't look like the Tylenol Mommy gives me," he said warily, pushing her hand away. "Is this for children?"

"Of course it's for children. Now take it," she ordered, thinking, *If he doesn't, I don't know what I'm going to do.*

He took the fragments from her palm and swallowed them one at a time, sipping milk from a straw. His expression was solemn. "Did you call Mommy and tell her we'd gone for a drive?" he asked. "She'll worry if you don't."

"I'll go do that right now." Instead, she went to the bathroom and splashed some cold water on her face. "Get a grip," she told the mirrored image, whose flushed cheeks seemed to belong to someone else.

She watched him finish his hamburger and fries. "Don't do that," she told him when he sucked air through his straw. "It's bad for your digestion." She scooped his refuse onto the tray and took it to the trash bin.

On the way to the car, he asked, "Did Mommy get mad?"

"No! Why should she?"

He hesitated for a moment, then shrugged his shoulders. "We don't really know you. That's why."

"But you're getting to know me, right?" She opened the passenger door. "That's all that counts."

He stood on the pavement and shifted his weight from one foot to the other. "I'm sleepy," he said, yawning. "I want to go back to the hotel and take a nap."

"Good idea," she said. "Hey. Why not crawl into the backseat? You can lie down and take a snooze while we're on the road."

He yawned again. "Snooze is a funny word."

When he continued to sleep past the dinner hour, she started to worry. What was the dosage of the pills? She couldn't remember. It had been listed on the bottle, which she'd put back in her friend's cosmetic case. The girl had chronic insomnia and might be on a large dose that could really harm a child. Maybe she should stop, get him out, walk him around. No, that would be too risky. She'd have to keep going till dark. They'd check into a motel. He'd sleep it off, and in the morning everything would be right as rain.

But what if it wasn't? What if she'd endangered his life? She should really have him looked at by a doctor, maybe someone in one of those sidewalk clinics. Of course, she'd have to give a fake name, but he'd still be asleep and wouldn't hear. Yes, she'd have to play it safe and have him seen. She'd take the next exit and pull into a gas station. They'd direct her to the nearest medical facility.

While she was getting gas, Paul sat up, rubbed his eyes, and said, "I'm cold. Where are we? I thought you said we were going back to the hotel." Then he kicked the back of the front seat and began to cry. "I want Mommy!" he wailed.

The attendant stuck his head in the window and said, "Ten bucks, lady. Whassa matter, kid? Past your bedtime?"

She took out her wallet and gave the attendant a ten-dollar bill. "He's really tired. We've been traveling all day. Is there a motel nearby?"

"Super 8 down the road."

"Mommy!" Paul screamed.

"Shut up," she whispered as they pulled away. She didn't want to treat him harshly, but if he was going to throw tantrums, she'd have to be firm. "If you don't shut up, you'll never see your mommy again," she said loudly.

He stopped crying.

She turned into the driveway of the Super 8. "Wait here," she told him. "I'm going to get us a room. You'll feel better once you're inside. And warmer."

Paul was quiet until they got inside. Then he started crying again. She grabbed his shoulders and shook him. "Take your things off and get into bed!" she ordered. When she lay down beside him, she could feel him trembling. *This isn't the way it was supposed to be,* she thought.

The next morning, while they were eating breakfast, she told him, "We're going to buy some new clothes today."

He said nothing.

"Eat your food. You want to feel good, don't you? To feel good, you have to eat."

"I don't like scrambled eggs."

"Drink your milk, then. Wait. Let me give you some more Tylenol. You look like you're coming down with something."

"Mommy doesn't give me pills."

"I'm not your mommy."

"I know," he said, starting to cry.

This time, she only had to raise her hand to make him stop. The fact that she was in control both pleased and saddened her. She could see that he was frightened. She looked around to see if anyone had noticed. Then she gave him a sleeping pill and watched him swallow.

She wondered if the effects were cumulative. She'd read that traces of certain drugs remain in your system for twenty-four to forty-eight hours after you take them. She wished she knew something about first aid. Then, if she got worried, she could examine his pupils for signs of an overdose.

In the next town, she found a small department store and bought herself a skirt, a blouse, a couple of pairs of underpants, some panty hose, and a sweater. She bought Paul a pair of jeans and a flannel shirt, some underwear, socks, and a windbreaker. He'd said he wanted a baseball cap, so she bought him one with the Red Sox logo he requested. She found a Walgreen's and purchased toiletries. She also bought a canvas duffel bag large enough to hold everything.

As she was about to leave the store she saw a set of small cars, which she bought as a surprise. She couldn't wait for him to wake up. She wanted him to be happy, but most of all, she wanted him to like her.

That night they stayed in a fancier motel. She let him eat whatever he wanted because this seemed to please him, and she didn't want to risk any scenes in the dining room.

After dinner they went back to their room and fell asleep watching cowboy movies. In the middle of the night she awoke to find him curled, like a kitten, at the bottom of the bed. For a while she sat up watching him, thinking about their future and what they might do with their lives once the running stopped.

The next morning, in the lobby of the motel as she settled her bill, she noticed the headlines in a local newspaper: "Bank Exec's Son Kidnapped at Resort." There, above the article, was Paul's photograph, and next to it a picture of his anguished parents. She skimmed the article, found her own name, and jammed the folded paper in her pocket. She picked up her credit card and left fifty cents for the paper in its place, then turned and walked quickly back to the room where she had left Paul asleep.

"Get up," she said, yanking back the covers and tugging at his arms. "We've got to get going." He opened his eyes and lay motionless on the bed. She struggled to dress him. "Come on, Paul, help me," she pleaded, noticing for the first time how much he resembled his mother. The newspaper said he was an only child. *Well, she can have another.* She struggled to pull on his shirt over his head, but his arms dangled at his sides. "Remember what I said about not seeing your mother?" she threatened, hoping to jolt him into cooperating.

He pushed her hands away. "I hate you!" he yelled. "You wicked witch!"

She could see her reflection in the mirror, red-faced, scary. He was right. She was wicked, and she didn't deserve him. She could imagine how it would hurt to lose a son. Imagine? She knew from experience.

By the time he was dressed, she'd made up her mind to let him go.

The Greyhound station was crowded with travelers. She figured she'd wait until he was safely in his seat before telling him he was going home. There was a clock on the wall and she watched it closely: twenty minutes until departure. "Stay with me, Paul," she urged. He was carrying his cars in a McDonald's Happy Meal carton.

"I have to go to the bathroom."

"Okay, okay. But hurry up. We don't want to miss our ride." She'd told him they were taking the bus back to the hotel because something had gone wrong with the car.

Ten minutes later she asked a teenager if he'd mind checking on her little boy. "He's wearing a blue jacket and a Red Sox cap. His name is Paul." She watched the tall, gangly kid with an earring and tattoos lope into the men's room. Endless minutes passed. What was taking him so long? She could feel her heart quicken. Anything could happen to a child these days, especially a good-looking boy like Paul.

When the teenager came out he said, "There's no kid in there now, lady. I looked all over."

If he'd come to any harm, it would be her fault. She'd allowed her eyes to wander for a few seconds as she perused the list of arrivals and departures, and in those few seconds Paul must have slipped by.

She realized she'd have to act quickly, so she hurried in the direction of the office of depot security. She would report that she'd seen a boy who looked like the banker's son leaving the men's room. She'd say she worries about children these days because there are so many dangers lurking in public places. Then she'd look at her watch. Were they through questioning her? she'd ask. Because if they were, her bus was scheduled to leave. No problem, they'd respond. They'd thank her for her trouble. And they would, of course, praise her for being so observant.

NEAR MOON

On this Boston Marathon Monday, Bernice Marie Weingarten is driving her father to his regular monthly appointment at the clinic outside the city. It's a mild day in mid-April, but Irving, cold all year round because of his sluggish heart, wears a Russian-style fake fur hat that dwarfs his face and a fake fur-trimmed storm coat two sizes too big for his shrinking frame. Turtlelike, he pokes his head out of his shell to check the traffic. "Okay, kiddo," he says. "You can get over in the left lane, but you'll have to step on the gas."

Lately Bernice has become reluctant to drive him places because he kibbitzes constantly. Now, as she struggles to retain her good humor, she reminds herself how glad she is to have him back among the living. When she got to his house earlier that morning, he was still in his pajamas, sitting on the edge of his bed, rubbing his eyes like a sleepy toddler. "Yo, Pop. It's me. Remember what day it is? It's the day we go to see Dr. Yan." Just thinking about the cardiologist gives her a thrill. Was it true Orientals didn't have any hair on their chests? She'd give anything to know. "Time to get dressed." Feeling a rush of tenderness, she unbuttoned Irving's pajama jacket and handed him his undershirt, which lay on his lap like spilled milk. "You're supposed to pull it over your head, Pop." She'd give anything to lie next to Yan and run her fingers over his nipples, those tiny islands in a sea of hairless flesh. Her father's bedroom smells ripe, echoing the morning bowel movement, a reminder that he sometimes forgets to tend to his personal hygiene—simple things like taking a shower every other day, or changing his underwear. Yan smells yummy, some kind of subtle cologne tinged with vanilla. Remembering this helped her overcome her nausea as she waited for her father to respond.

When he finally came around, he left the shirt bunched under his armpits for her to straighten. "Now what? Hey. Let's go casual today. How about a jersey? No pesky buttons on a jersey." He stuck his arms up obediently and she jammed the jersey over his head. "There are stains all over this, Pop. Don't you use that laundry spray I gave you?" When she pulled off his pajama bottoms, she tried not to stare at his plum-colored, wrinkled genitals. "You want your longies, Pop?" She waited for him to pull them up, which he finally did, in lackluster fashion. "You want these trousers? You want suspenders? Brown or black socks? Your Nikes or your Easy Spirits?" He'll have youthful-looking yuppie feet at least, she thought as she laced his sneakers tight and pulled him to a standing position.

In the car she said, "Here. Let me fasten your seat belt."

He yanked the coupling out of her hands. "What am I, a baby? You should let me drive. You know how you hate the traffic."

"Very funny, Pop." For the first month or so after she stopped him from driving, he was angry and got even by calling cabs at all hours and never telling her where he was going. Then he seemed to work things out. Now, when they travel together, he's often cheerfully talkative. As always, his favorite topic is Anna, his wife, who died a year ago. "We were like two turtledoves cooing away," he will say. "You wouldn't believe how romantic we were. Your mother was so beautiful." Bernice thinks about the sepia snapshots in their early albums, pictures somebody took of them at the beach with their heads together like Kewpie dolls, or the one in which Anna is kneeling and bending forward, showing cleavage, and Irving is kneeling behind her, his hands resting firmly on her shoulders, his cheek near hers. Over the years she'd rarely thought of them as lovers. "When we went out, I could feel the fellows all looking at her and thinking, What a lucky guy. And I was a lucky guy." She hears the catch in his voice and responds in kind by swallowing hard.

Five minutes later he's asleep, his chin resting on his chest, the back of his neck stretched, it seems, almost to the point of snapping. Sometimes, when she stops in to see him after lunch, she finds him asleep in his chair like this, with his soap opera playing to an empty house.

She wishes she could trust him to run his household, but these days Irving forgets to turn off the burners, lock the doors, take out the garbage, brush his teeth. If she didn't check up on him three times a day, who knows what else he'd forget? Fortunately, she lives only a mile away. A friend wonders why they don't combine households. Bernice replies, "If he lived with me, my life would be over." As it is, her life isn't what she'd like it to be. She'd really like to take a cruise, meet some men. But she can't even go across town without worrying about him. She's tried hiring Home Helpers, but they just sat around watching television while Irving climbed ladders to fix things, fell down, and concussed. Sometimes she wonders why she ever encouraged her parents to move to New Hampshire.

Each morning, when she calls to check on him, he drops the receiver and says, "Oops, butterfingers," a phrase that used to amuse her, but which now serves as a reminder of how crippled his hands have become. His swollen, wavy fingers look like little Cuban bananas, the ones you fry up for dessert. "You'll bring the paper?" he wants to know, because the paper is part of his morning ritual, whether or not he reads it. While he was still driving, he used to get it himself. He'd pull his old Lincoln Continental out of the garage, brushing the wall he parked too close to the day before. "So who cares about splintered wood?" he used to say. If only it'd been just the wood! One day he almost hit his neighbor, who was walking her dogs, and the next day he grazed the little mail van with his rear bumper. By that time, he'd shrunk so much that approaching motorists must have wondered who, if anyone, was behind the wheel. Bernice dreamed about children being squashed flat in the supermarket parking lot, the imprints of Michelins burned onto their flesh. Then one day, when she was his passenger, he turned into the path of an oncoming truck and just barely missed killing them both. She knew then that the time had come for her to revoke his driving privileges.

She decided to sweeten the poison by taking him to his favorite Chinese restaurant. When she called to invite him to lunch she joked, "How about letting me provide the limo?"

Clunk. "Oops, butterfingers." Pause. "You don't like it when I drive, do you? It makes you nervous."

"Well, I worry about the other people, Pop."

Pause. "You think I shouldn't drive."

There it was: Before she'd even had a chance to soften the blow with Sweet and Pungent Pork, he'd raised the issue. But then she remembered that Irving had always been a reader of minds. "Can we talk about this later? There's someone at the door," she lied, not wanting to deliver her ultimatum over the phone.

At the restaurant, things went better than she had expected. Since he'd anticipated her request, he'd obviously thought about how he'd respond. "I can understand how you'd feel about my driving," he began. "But honey, you gotta try to see it my way. If I can't drive, what can I do? I'll be a prisoner in my own house. I'll have to wait for you to do everything for me. Now, at least I can run my own errands. You see what I mean?"

Bernice looked across the table and noticed that Irving had managed, after just one forkful, to spill sticky sauce down the front of his already stained shirt. She wanted to scold him for being messy, but at times like this she had to remind herself that she was the child, not the parent. Basically, she understood and respected his need to remain independent, but she also worried about accidents and what others would say. "Will you excuse me, Pop?" She slid out of the banquette to scoot into the ladies' room, hoping to buy some time.

She peed leisurely, then washed her hands twice. The last thing she did was splash water on her face and blot it with paper towels. In the mirror, her image stared back, and she thought she looked brave and resolute.

Back at the table, she watched Irving toy with his swizzle stick and avoid her gaze. After a couple of minutes, he said, "They don't have that fried rice your mom used to love, the stuff that had little pieces of shrimp and ham in it. She used to call it fancy-shmancy rice. Remember?"

At the sound of this mournful recollection, Bernice's resolve faded. With Anna's ghost hovering over the table, it would be even harder for her to lay down the law. But she was determined to push on. She reached across the table, took hold of his banana fingers, and squeezed them gently to show him she cared, and that she understood. "I'm sorry, Pop. Driving is out. We'll sell the car. Then maybe, with some of the money, you'll go to Florida and visit Seymour." Seymour was his bridge buddy of bygone years, his boyhood pal, the only other surviving member of their gang of four from high school.

Irving looked at her in shock. "Have you forgotten Seymour's in a home? You can't stay with people who live in a home! He only has one room, and he shares that with someone. You wanna know something, Bernice? Growing old sucks!" He spoke loudly and pounded the table for emphasis, but the worst was yet to come: He started to cry. "I wish I could be with Anna. I'd give anything to be with my Anna!"

The couple sitting in the booth behind them suddenly stopped talking. Bernice came from a long line of people who made scenes in restaurants, and knew what would follow. Irving would continue, his quavery voice escalating, until he had everyone's attention. "Jesus, Pop, keep your voice down," she whispered. Miraculously, he responded by stifling his sobs. She found herself overwhelmed by pity and close to tears herself. If only she could think of something that would make him feel better! Then it came to her: "Hey. How about sending Seymour the plane fare so he can come and visit? You guys could hang out, like old times. Maybe even go to the track. They have a bus that goes there," she added quickly, not wanting him to get any ideas that she'd let him off the hook about giving up his driving. But Irving just sat there, morosely sipping his Scotch and sniffling. After a while he blew his nose noisily and said, "How do we know they don't have that rice? Just because they don't put it on the menu. We could ask!" And he put his pinkies in his mouth and whistled for the waiter, who jumped as if he'd been shot.

Later, she watched him pore over the check while she cracked her fortune cookie. "You have an irresistible personality," she read. "Yeah, right." She reached for the little slip of paper he held in his hands. "Lemme see yours, Pop." She watched him roll up his fortune, stick it in his mouth, and swallow. "Oh my God, Pop," she said in horror. "You ate it!"

He smiled. "Whatsa matter, Bernice? Don't you like secrets?"

She didn't know what to think. Half the time he acted bizarre, but the other half he seemed normal, or nearly so. She knew he wasn't as sharp about money as he used to be; for instance, he'd forgotten to add enough for a tip. She waited until he wouldn't notice, then slipped four dollars under her plate. As they left, she could hear the couple behind them laughing. She wanted to slap their faces. Someday you'll do weird things too, she wanted to tell them. Then see how funny you think it is.

The rest of the afternoon crawled on without further discussion of the issue, but she knew he knew she meant business, and she trusted him to cooperate. It wasn't in her to push for the sale of the car, so it remained in his garage, a sad old warhorse yearning for action. It wasn't as if Irving would get a lot of money for it, because the car wasn't old enough to be a classic and there was quite a bit of rust on the body. So its main value was as a sentimental relic of Irv and Anna's twilight years, of the many wonderful trips they took in that car, which they named Gilda after the Rita Hayworth film. And the name suited the car, elegant and sensual. It was a car that might have belonged to well-heeled Wasps in the Hamptons; in fact, that was probably the reason he'd bought it in the first place. Bernice couldn't think why she'd never figured it out before.

The renowned clinic has a doorman who will bring a wheelchair to the car, so that Irving can ride into his appointment in style. Bernice pries him out of the front seat and watches him unfold slowly, like a flower shot in time-lapse. "Easy does it, fella," the doorman says. Instinctively, Irving reaches for his wallet, but she stops him. In his world, all those who serve must be rewarded, but tipping is self-righteously discouraged here. They watch the car jock jump behind the wheel and drive away. Irving shakes his head. "Valet parking at the doctor's. What's next?"

Inside the cavernous lobby old people congregate, the lame and the near-blind seeking to be healed. He motions for her to stop pushing the chair. They pause on the outskirts of the crowd. "What is it? Do you have to go to the bathroom?" she asks. He shakes his head no, then nods yes, then no again. "What is it, Pop?" she repeats. For an instant she thinks he honestly doesn't know, or if he does, he can't think how to tell her. He has these funny times when he fades out, but as long as he fades in again she figures she can cope. A minute or so passes before he speaks. "This is Tuesday," he says confidently. "And I'm at the clinic." He looks up at her and smiles. "Right?"

In the doctor's office, Irving seems so, well, normal that Bernice feels silly recounting the morning's ups and downs. Dr. Yan listens patiently, and then explains: "Your father suffers these transient ischemic attacks caused by a temporary deficiency of blood due to constricted vessels. When the blood doesn't get to the brain, confusion results. Not to worry. This doesn't mean he's having a stroke. In most cases, it's only temporary, and no permanent damage is done." The doctor reaches over to touch her hand in a gesture of reassurance, and she inhales vanilla bean essence and thinks about touching his nipples. Ooh. Is there a Mrs. Yan? She wishes she knew.

Later, when they're in the cafeteria, Irving revisits the twilight zone and holds up the line. Bernice guides him toward the stack of trays. "Hey, Pop," she says gently. "Do you want something cold? Something hot?" He ignores her, and shuffles along. People stare. "Can you manage this tray, Pop?" she asks, selecting a chicken salad sandwich, a dish of orange Jell-O with fruit, a cup of hot water, and a tea bag. Irving stops in front of the macaroni and cheese. His tray tips, but a young nurse catches it just in time. "Hey, Pop, come on," Bernice pleads. "We're holding up the line."

Suddenly, he wakes from his trance to peel a twenty from his money clip and says loudly, "My treat." Fives, tens, and ones go flying, and Bernice is down on her hands and knees scooping up bills, thinking he belongs in a nursing home where someone else can keep track of him every minute of the day.

On the ride back, she relents, of course, and decides she'll let him stay in his own place a little longer.

As he sleeps, she listens to Public Radio. Terry Gross is interviewing a jazz musician who plays trumpet like he's being chased by the devil. Bernice allows her thoughts to swirl at a dizzy pace with the music: Gilda must go, something will have to be done about Irving (though she can't think what), she needs to get away but she's not sure she'd like a cruise—too many lonely women desperate to dance with the crew. And what about Seymour's visit? A good time for him to come would be when the car goes. "Pop," she prods softly, knowing he's just floating above the surface of sleep, "did you ever write Seymour about coming up to visit?"

Irving the turtle raises his head and turns to look at her with hooded, milky eyes. "I guess you don't know that Seymour died last week, Anna"—he often calls her by her mother's name. "I heard it from his daughter. No big deal. He went in his sleep. Lucky bastard, I say." The turtle disappears and in its place is a little old man wearing a fake fur hat, who takes out his handkerchief and wipes his eyes.

Bernice doesn't know how to respond, so she waits for him to recover, which he does in a couple of minutes.

"Did I ever tell you the story of how I met your mother? It was Seymour who introduced us. I bet you never knew that." In his voice is just an echo of the emotion he must be feeling as the only survivor of the gang of four. The car goes forward propelled by Bernice's foot on the accelerator, Irving's voice, the wild musings of a frenetic trumpeter. She thinks of the marathon runners cresting Heartbreak Hill, pushing toward the finish, urged on by the cheering throngs, and of the stragglers looking half-dead who fall into the arms of race attendants. What must it feel like to almost finish the course, she wonders.

In the distance, the sky is ribboned layers of pink, gray, blue, and gold, a harbinger of wonders yet to come. Tonight they'll see a full moon close up. The meteorologists have been preparing everyone for days. Just thinking about it is giving her goose bumps.

That evening they share a simple supper—macaroni and cheese, green beans with almonds, ice cream for dessert—his favorite meal, though not one his doctor would approve. Irving's at the microwave the whole time, pressing buttons and smiling, once more in command. Bernice wonders when the next little stroke will occur. Before it does, she thinks, I'd better check out the refrigerator. "Hey, Pop. What did you have that was green? How long ago did you buy this cheese? When did you open this bottle of wine?" She might as well be talking to herself, because he's in his recliner watching CNN, so she dumps anything that looks suspicious and makes a quick trip out to the garage with two big bags of garbage and a plastic sack full of recyclables. Gilda sits there in all her splendor. Something will have to be done, Bernice thinks, but not tonight when the moon is full and closer than it's ever been to earth.

She walks out to the middle of the small backyard that Anna used to cram with vegetables and flowers. Since her passing, the grass and weeds have taken over, but Bernice always remembers the way it used to look. Neighbors would have been glad to pay Anna for the big juicy tomatoes she always gave away, rosy beauties that gave off a subtle perfume and tasted like ambrosia. Anna Marcello, born into a big Italian family known for its gardening skills, loved growing those tomatoes, along with the lumpy Hubbard squash, lush dahlias, anemones, and huge bearded irises that dwarfed everyone else's. Her garden was her link with the heritage she left behind when she married a skinny little Jew from the Bronx and created a child who would always feel the pull of two cultures.

Bernice thinks her mother would have loved a moon so large it looks fake. For the first time, she can really see a person in there, two eyes, a nose, and a mouth, and that person is looking through her into the house where Irving sits dozing and watching the news that never stops. On the television screen the winners of the marathon are smiling as if the moment will last forever, and their fists are raised in triumph to the skies. She starts to shiver and thinks she should get a jacket, but instead stands transfixed by the near moon's stare on this crisp spring night. There will come a day when she will have only herself to think about, but for now, there's Irving with his transient ischemic attacks, living half the time in a place neither of them recognizes. Thinking about how he must feel terrifies her. The least she can do is hold his hand, comfort him, stay with him until the end. The camera pans to the left, where two spectators are dragging a limp racer to the finish line, and she sees her father's face, reluctant to continue but determined to get there just the same.

THE GO-BETWEEN

Now that we've been reunited with our old friends in Belgium, I'm trying my best to understand their situation. It's bizarre, though. For instance, I find myself fancying that Jean-Paul is flirting with me. With me! I'm hardly a beauty, and he's past the age of flirting (although I'd never suggest that to him), yet right now he's saying things like, "You look splendid! You haven't changed at all. You still have such beautiful skin," while Marty and Elsa are in the kitchen of our rented flat struggling with a reluctant wine cork.

"Why, thank you," I say. I imagine I'm blushing. I want to blush. Instead, I force myself to remain businesslike, and ask primly, "When are we going to meet this new wife of yours?"

Suddenly his mood shifts. "That won't be possible," he says curtly. "It would upset Elsa too much." Then, changing the subject, he asks, "What's keeping those two, anyway? The cork must have crumbled, and they must be having to use cheesecloth to strain the wine!" He gets up to investigate.

While I'm alone, I pick up yesterday's *Tribune,* and scan articles about things that happened days ago at home: a hurricane, Reagan's skin cancer, Rock Hudson's death. Here, the emphasis is still on the passing of Simone Signoret, who died last week. Wasn't *Room at the Top* about an older woman who was jilted by a young lover? But

Elsa and Jean-Paul are the same age. Or are they? His new German wife is reputed to be fifteen, maybe twenty years younger than he.

It was Marty's idea to return to Brussels and rent an apartment here for the month of September. I remember exactly when the subject first came up, and the conversation that resulted in his reaching for the address book I keep in my desk. He started leafing through the indexed pages, looking up at me over the rims of the half-glasses that make him look slightly stupid.

"I know their names are still in there," I said. "I send them a card every Christmas." I got impatient. I pulled the book away from him and turned right to the page with the names of our friends written carefully in black ink. In the early days of our marriage, I was precise about keeping records, but as the years went by, my standards slipped. Most pages became marred with hastily made corrections, some deletions made by crossing out and others by slopping on correction fluid and not waiting long enough for it to dry. But Elsa and Jean-Paul's address stayed the same all through the years. "Here it is," I said triumphantly. "A beautiful apartment, remember? There was a terrace with wrought-iron chairs and a little stone statue of Eros."

Marty looked at me, tilting his chin down and rolling his eyes up. He's so vain. He'll do anything to avoid wearing glasses all the time. "Didn't you give somebody their names last year? Wasn't some college pal of yours supposed to look them up? She might be able to tell us if they've moved or not."

"I don't think she ever called them. You know how these things are—people get shy about taking the initiative. If I had done more—I don't know, maybe written or even called Elsa first—then the ice would have been broken."

Marty got up from his chair, took his glasses off, and gave me a hug. He kissed me on the neck. "My little go-between," he said, "always trying to make things right," but I was too distracted to respond. I was thinking of an evening spent with Elsa and Jean-Paul many years earlier, the night before we flew home. Elsa had cooked

Marty's favorite dish, duck in pears, and we had somehow worked our way through three bottles of wine. It was September, warm for that time of year, so we had eaten our meal on the terrace. I remember there was a gentle breeze that made the edge of Elsa's linen tablecloth flutter, made her soft blond hair seem even softer, like the gentle wispy curls of angels in a Van Eyck triptych. There was an angelic quality about her in those days, an entrancing air that made her seem fragile until you saw her swim or play tennis. It was then you sensed how physically strong she really was. They had always seemed the ideal couple: she, small and slender, with slightly bronzed skin; he, tall and dark, as ruggedly handsome as she was delicately pretty. They both had smiles that dazzled. Marty and I would have felt quite inferior if it hadn't been for the unique nature of our friendship; despite the circumstances that separated us, we had much in common.

So it was that this particular evening was tinged with sadness, because we were leaving the next day to return to the States, Marty having completed his medical studies at the University of Louvain and I having completed most of the background work for my master's thesis on the use of symbols in Flemish painting. Marty and I had met at a New Year's party given by the American ambassador; six months later we were lovers, planning to be married. Jean-Paul, a physician, had been Marty's lab preceptor the year before, and the two of them had become friends, initially because of their mutual love for tennis, which Elsa and I shared.

That warm September evening as we sat on the terrace of their beautiful apartment, Jean-Paul, normally cheerful and talkative, was pensive. He sat quietly looking out across the tops of the chestnut trees that lined their avenue. He seemed not to be listening to our conversation. In a way, I could understand his distraction, because we looked out on a scene of utter peace and tranquillity, and it seemed a shame to shatter the mood with idle talk. The trees were illuminated from the ground, and when the wind rustled the leaves, they seemed to shimmer in the night.

Occasionally, chestnuts would fall to the pavement with a muffled plop. I reached over to touch his shoulder lightly, letting him know I understood, and he responded in the most extraordinary way, by taking both of my hands in his hands and kissing them. The gesture brought tears to my eyes, so I excused myself, hurrying to the bathroom, where I pretended to use the toilet. When I looked into the mirror, I could see Elsa's lace-trimmed peignoir hanging on a hook. I looked down at my hands and thought them thoroughly unkissable.

By the time I returned to the table, the mood had changed, and Jean-Paul was offering cognac, which I refused. Marty, however, indulged himself, and when we left their apartment after midnight, I had to help him in and out of the elevator and down the front steps to our little Citroën. I drove through quiet streets to our place, perhaps three kilometers from theirs. When I pulled up next to the curb in front of our building, Marty was asleep and I was reluctant to wake him. For a while I just sat there, hoping he'd come to. I looked across the street at the little store where I had done my daily shopping for the past year, saw that the metal screen was pulled down over the shopfront, and wondered how long it had taken them to move all the produce from the stands outside to the shelves inside, a process that would be repeated in reverse the next morning, in about six hours. Soon the bakery trucks would deliver long brown loaves of crusty bread, and the milkmen would arrive with their clanking bottles. Soon dogs would bark, and shopkeepers would lift their screens and roll out their awnings in preparation for another day of trading. Meanwhile, my husband-to-be slept beside me in the front seat of the battered old car we would be leaving behind when we returned to the States.

About a year later, when we had been married six months, Marty attended a medical conference in Montreal. When he returned, he told me he had seen Jean-Paul.

"And Elsa?" I asked. "How is she? Pretty as ever?"

"She wasn't there. At least I didn't see her," Marty said. "Jean-Paul was keeping company with an American woman, some research whiz from Detroit. They acted as if they really knew each other," he added.

"You mean in the biblical sense?" I asked, beginning to laugh.

"Yeah," Marty said. "They seemed to be on intimate terms. And the strange thing was, Jean-Paul acted as if he hardly recognized me."

"Maybe he was embarrassed. Was she good-looking, this research whiz?" I remember asking.

"She was pretty in a well-organized sort of way. You know. Dressed just so, and with the right amount of makeup."

"I didn't know you noticed such things," I teased. "Didn't you at least call him in his room after you'd seen them?"

"I figured it was none of my business. The way I look at it, if the guy wants to screw around, it's his affair, not mine. Personally, if I had a wife who looked like Elsa, I'd be afraid *she* was playing around."

"Elsa would never sleep with someone else," I insisted, feeling I owed her that small allegiance.

"Did she tell you that?"

"Yes," I lied. In reality, the subject had never come up.

"Well, you were a fool to believe her."

Of course he would stick up for Jean-Paul, I remember thinking, but I know he's wrong about Elsa.

It was a long time before I thought about her again. Oh, there was the usual polite and meaningless exchange of Christmas greetings, but never anything more from her than a scrawled signature on a printed card—her name and his, so we assumed they had survived their crises as we, over the years, had survived ours. Then, just before we left for Europe, I received a letter from her with only the barest of details: There had been a divorce; Jean-Paul had married a German woman; yet, Elsa insisted, she and Jean-Paul were still the best of friends.

∞

The idea of people no longer married to each other behaving as if they still are is disturbing to me, especially since I know how Jean-Paul's marriage has affected Elsa. Yet here they sit across the table from us, smiling and teasing and carrying on as if nothing has changed. For instance, Elsa orders lobster bisque and Jean-Paul says, "You know you hate lobster bisque," and so she orders pâté instead. Or Jean-Paul orders the apéritif of the house and Elsa says, "You know you don't like Campari and orange juice, so why not order Scotch and soda?" and he does.

Later in the evening, he says to her, "I see you're wearing the earrings I gave you last Christmas," and she smiles.

The earrings he gave her last Christmas! For Christ's sake, he's been married to the German woman for two years. One has to wonder what she thinks of all this. I can't stand it any longer, so I excuse myself and go to the bathroom.

Elsa follows. "Are you okay?" she asks. "Not upset by anything you ate, I hope. We think the food is marvelous here."

"Oh, it is," I agree, wondering if they come here often. "It reminds me of the place the four of us used to go."

"I was thinking of that place only the other day," Elsa says dreamily, perching on the edge of the dressing table. "We had some good times, didn't we?" Tears spill. She blots her eyes carefully with a tissue.

I chide myself for bringing up the past, when she should be learning to deal with the present. "I didn't mean to upset you," I mumble.

Elsa puts her hand on my arm and presses slightly. I can feel the warmth of her skin through the sleeve of my blouse and instinctively I pull away. "You mustn't think that I've forgotten those happier times," she says softly.

"If it helps, I think he's behaved like a bastard."

She purses her lips. "Oh, you mustn't think badly of him. He feels very guilty, you know." She fingers the skirt of her flowered-print dress, a dress that on anyone else would look like a flirty schoolgirl's prom outfit but only serves to accent Elsa's femininity.

"Of course he does! Why else would he keep seeing you?" I blurt out.

"Why darling, I'm surprised at you. Isn't it perfectly evident?"

Bewildered, I can only shake my head.

"He still loves me!" She says it triumphantly, and before I can choke out a response, she is leading me back to the table. Marty and Jean-Paul stand up in unison, like a pair of puppets jerked to their feet, in welcome.

Later that evening, as Marty and I prepare for bed, I tell him what Elsa has said, and he responds. "I think she's partially correct. But only partially. It's clear he isn't about to leave the German woman."

"We can't go on calling her 'the German woman.' "

"Why not? Elsa calls her the Kraut," Marty says, laughing. "I bet she calls her a few other things, too." We turn down the covers together. "I bet she's a knockout, a beautiful babe. God knows she'd have to be," he says as he pulls the nubby orange drapes partway across the window, and slides open one panel so the Indian summer air can unstuff the room.

Our lovemaking is swift, accomplished with minimal effort on both parts, not altogether satisfactory. In a little while, Marty is asleep. I lie on my back with my hands straight at my sides, like an Egyptian princess. Scenes at dinner keep coming back to distract me. When we drank a champagne toast with dessert, Jean-Paul raised his glass and said, "To old times," and I felt like kicking him. How he must love being adored by two women! It seems to me there's no justice where women like Elsa are concerned.

In the middle of the night or, more correctly, close to dawn, the woman in the upstairs apartment screams out in pain or passion. I know her husband or lover beats her, usually in the morning, because I can hear him slapping her around. The sound of her crying comes through the vent in our bathroom ceiling. I've thought of speaking to the concierge, but for all I know the concierge *is* that woman. Her face isn't bruised, but perhaps he's careful to hit her where the bruises won't show. Now she's moaning again, and the sound of her voice is strangely arousing. I close my eyes and imagine I'm making love to Jean-Paul. He is caressing my breasts with those big, strong hands of his, hands roped with veins like Michelangelo's *David.* My nipples are erect. Other parts of me are soft and liquid, demanding, fiercely insisting on penetration, but not quite yet; wait, I beg, just a second more, I promise it won't be long—and in spite of knowing that I'm dreaming, I can feel the tension in my body as it prepares for release.

Afterward, when there's not a sound from upstairs, I fall deeply asleep.

The next morning, Marty leaves early to visit one of his old professors in Louvain. When I call Elsa and suggest we go shopping on the Avenue Louise, she mentions an outdoor café as a meeting place, and we agree on a time. At lunch, I tell her about the woman upstairs whose husband or lover beats her. "That's one way of being cruel," she says, giving me a deep look charged with meaning. Changing the subject, she asks if I've seen some mutual friends who live in Massachusetts. She says "Matchashooshits," and I laugh. Once more the mood lightens, and we enjoy our lunch of cold shrimp, tomatoes, crusty bread, and wine.

Later, she buys a lovely cashmere sweater and charges it to Jean-Paul. I look at her in surprise. "He lets you do that?"

"Of course. I told you he feels guilty."

I will never understand this arrangement.

When Elsa and I part, it's mid-afternoon. At first I think of going downtown to a museum, but then I decide to take a walk through the Bois de la Cambre, the big park that is near Elsa's apartment and not far from ours. While I am strolling around, I think I see Marty sitting in an outdoor café, but how could it be Marty? So many men wear their hair like that, and in khaki raincoats they all look alike.

Rather than pass by and possibly embarrass myself and others by staring, I turn quickly in the other direction.

When Marty isn't back by seven, I mix myself a drink and turn on the BBC news. Riots have broken out in the London suburbs. On another channel, a Belgian chef shows me how to stuff quail. I turn off the TV and slide open the door that leads out to our little balcony, then I hear Marty coming in the front door.

Right away I can tell he's been drinking. "I hope you haven't had dinner, because I'm starving," I say.

He puts his coat back on. "Well then, what are we waiting for?" he says, grinning, cheerfully obliging though unsteady on his feet. I reach out to help him get his balance and catch a whiff of a perfume whose scent is vaguely familiar.

On the way out of the building, we pass the concierge. "Did you notice if her face is bruised?" I whisper.

"What the fuck are you talking about?"

He pilots me down the street and into a restaurant we've often thought of patronizing. "M'sieur-m'dame," the waiter chants as he leads us to a table in the corner, "apéritif?" Marty nods. Without consulting me he has committed us to crème de cassis and champagne, which I don't like. "Bon," says the waiter, and his face lightens with just the suggestion of a smile.

I am prepared to have a terrible time.

"So," Marty says when we have finished our meal in silence. "Tell me what you did all day." He is looking at a young woman who is sitting alone at the next table. She's pretty in a contemporary way, with her hair spiked and colored in punk fashion.

"I went shopping with Elsa. Then she had an appointment, so I went back to the flat and waited for you." I know he isn't listening. Any minute, the girl will respond by returning his stare, or by getting up and leaving. In an effort to distract Marty, I fool around with my spoon, first sticking it in my coffee, then taking it out and tapping it against the saucer, an annoying gesture I know he can't stand.

It works. Irritated, he puts his hand over mine. "Why do you do that when you know it pisses me off?" he asks. The girl gets up and leaves the restaurant. Marty signals to the waiter by pretending to write on the palm of his left hand with the index finger of his right hand, a universal pantomime. The waiter snaps to and brings us our check. He flicks crumbs from our tablecloth with a little linen towel. Here we are in a simple neighborhood tavern, and the waiter is dressed formally and he uses a linen towel. That's Belgium for you.

"M'sieur-m'dame," the waiter drones as we leave.

When we let ourselves into the flat, the phone is ringing. It's Elsa, sounding upset. She wants me to come over for tea the next day. "Did you have a nice dinner?" she asks. "I had tuna fish from a can."

I replace the receiver. "Elsa wants me to come for tea tomorrow," I tell Marty. "Girl talk. Do you mind?"

He shrugs. "She's your friend. Do as you like." Then he goes into the bathroom to brush his teeth. I can hear him flossing, yanking the tape from his teeth with a vigor that comes with sobriety. He'll go straight to bed and I'll be stuck lying there beside him, waiting for the show to start upstairs.

On the way to Elsa's apartment, I stop at the florist to buy her some cut flowers. "C'est pour offrir?" the proprietor asks as she trims the stems of the painted daisies I have chosen. I nod yes, it's for someone else. Accordingly, she wraps the flowers in cellophane, folds down the top flap and fastens it with a pink bow and a silver sticker bearing the name of the shop. Then she gives the bouquet a little pat for good luck and hands it to me. I move aside to make room for the next customer, a handsome young woman in a print dress who speaks French with a German accent.

Halfway to Elsa's building, I look up to see the edge of the awning that marks the penthouse Jean-Paul now shares with his second wife, and it hits me. The woman in the florist's shop is the Kraut! Marty will say I'm being silly, but I know I'm right, and now she's going into Jean-Paul's building, which proves I'm right. She's not as pretty as Elsa, but she has a certain style. She has purchased a pot of chrysanthemums, which will look nice on their terrace. My heart is beating fast with the excitement of discovery.

"Well," says Elsa. She is standing in the doorway of her apartment framed by the afternoon sunlight that floods her living room. She has cut her hair. Why haven't I noticed it before? No more delicate wisps. This new style is more chic, more becoming to an older woman, more youthful. The Kraut wears her hair shoulder-length, with bangs. She is much younger than Elsa. "How sweet of you to bring my favorite flowers!" Elsa says. She takes the bouquet out of my hands and begins to undo the cellophane. "The color is perfect in my hallway, don't you agree?" Elsa's hands are slim and delicate; the Kraut has hands that are broad and functional. Marty will say that I couldn't possibly have noticed, but I did.

"Why don't we sit on the terrace? It's hot, but the sun is pleasant at this time of year," Elsa says.

I follow her out onto the terrace, and we sit on small wrought-iron chairs, possibly the same chairs we sat on when we dined on the penthouse terrace all those years ago. Jean-Paul must have kept the table, because this one is just a tiny round affair with a glass top, really all Elsa needs in this smaller space. I notice she still has the statue. "Tea?" she asks. "Or would you prefer a vodka tonic? I myself think it's a bit early for vodka tonic."

I tell her tea will be fine.

"Do you take lemon? I'm afraid I've no milk," she says, setting down a small tray. "I've been a naughty girl. I've bought some pastries, and you must help me eat them or I shall get terribly fat!" The old Elsa, coy and vain, shines through for a moment. I see she has brought out two little tarts, one lemon and one chocolate. "You choose," she says, but before I can say a word, she quickly puts the chocolate one on my plate. She hands me a small silver fork engraved with her married initials, and I think, *Of course she has managed to keep the silver.* We eat in silence. She pours the tea and offers me a slice of lemon. Twice she gets up to go to the railing, looks down, then comes back to the little table.

Finally I ask, "Are you feeling better? You sounded pretty upset when you called last night."

"Oh, forget about it—it was nothing. I had too much cognac. I should not have disturbed you. Shall we," and here she pauses to reach across the table and clasp my hands in an intimate gesture of friendship, "simply forget it?"

I slip my hands from hers. "Of course," I say, although I know there's more to this than she's letting on. She stands up again and crosses in front of me, and I realize that her perfume is the same scent I smelled on Marty's skin the other night. "Do you mind if I use your phone?" I ask abruptly, feeling nauseous.

Elsa nods dreamily. "Usually she goes out at this time of day to do her errands. Sometimes she brings back flowers. I haven't seen her today, though. Perhaps they're away. He takes her with him on business trips." I watch her fingers, like butterflies, flutter up to her throat. Her expression shifts from melancholy to impatience. "What am I thinking of, going on like this? Of course you can use the phone!" She pushes my shoulders gently, turns me around, and marches me into the hallway. There is a pressure in her touch that stings. When she pauses to ruffle the petals of the flowers I've brought her, I figure she is stalling for time. For an instant, I think she is going to tell me the truth, but then we continue into her bedroom, where a rose-colored telephone sits prettily on a small mahogany bedside table. "Wasn't Marty going out of town today?" she asks, and for the first time I notice how disgustingly adorable his name sounds when she says it: *Martee.* I wonder if this is some alibi they've concocted, then I look down and can't believe what I see: On the message pad Elsa has doodled the letter M. She's standing in the doorway waiting to see what I'll do, not suspecting I know. She's taken time to embellish the M carefully, as one might embroider the initials of a loved one on a linen pillowcase. What a fool they must think I am!

"Ah yes," I say, turning to face her. "Now I remember. He's going back to Louvain to see that professor. They can't seem to get enough of each other's company. Almost like lovers, wouldn't you say?" I look at her in such a way there can be no doubt I know everything.

She turns and walks quickly back to the balcony, with me following so close behind that I almost step on the heels of her shoes. Then, while she watches me with those beautiful big blue eyes, I pick up the statue of Eros and send that chubby little winged fucker flying over the balcony railing to the street below, where it narrowly misses hitting the roof of Jean-Paul's Mercedes and smashes into a million pieces, each big enough to wound somebody for life.

NOW LET US ALL GIVE THANKS

Jenny's fifteenth birthday was coming up, so Ellen planned a trip to the mall that Saturday, thinking it would be a good way for them to spend some time together. Besides, Jenny was going to Bermuda with her father in a couple of weeks and she needed some new things to wear. It would be the first time he had taken her on vacation since the divorce, and Jenny seemed both excited and anxious.

Ellen stood outside JCPenney and watched Jenny drift away into the crowd. The girl wore her straight brown hair long, with two skinny braids at either side. When she walked, they shifted from side to side in a graceful, fluid motion. She wore Levis, white Reeboks, and a Gap turtleneck sweater, the costume of the moment, and when she swung her shoulder pouch it almost brushed the floor. Jenny loved clothes, unlike her older sister Karen, who dressed comfortably and, much like their mother, never spent more than she absolutely had to on clothing. When Karen came home from college, she practiced the piccolo that used to be Ellen's in her bedroom with the door closed, but the piercing notes still penetrated all the still corners of the house, driving Jenny crazy. Since Karen had entered college, she and Ellen had become close, sharing an interest in classical music. As far as Jenny was concerned, classical music was for nerds, and anybody who played the piccolo needed to have her head examined.

Ellen entered a sporting goods store and walked over to a circular rack where men's warm-ups were displayed. She chose a light blue jacket with a white stripe on the collar and sleeves and a pair of matching pants, just the outfit she had been looking for. When she took it over to the counter, she was met by a salesman who reminded her of someone she'd known years before. Then she decided she must be mistaken—this man was thinner, and he wore a beard. Of course she had changed also, which might account for the fact that he didn't recognize her—assuming he was the person she used to know. It was all very confusing. She stood there staring down at the counter, not knowing what to do next. "Something I can help you with?" he asked, and she was even more perplexed because this man had the same soft, medium-register voice, the same almost musical way of speaking as her former lover. "Cash or charge?"

Ellen handed over her Visa and wondered if her name would seem familiar to him. She watched his face for any sign of recognition, but he remained politely aloof as he waited for authorization, then handed her the slip to sign. "Hope your husband likes the suit," he said, turning his attention to a pile of clothing that needed to be sorted.

As she walked out of the store, she realized she was hoping he'd come to his senses and follow her, but the solitary sound of her heels clicking against the mall pavement told her otherwise. Over the years she'd had occasional fantasies that she'd run into him and they'd resume their affair. In reality, she'd opted to stay with Brad. Of course, her lover had never come right out and said that if she left her husband, he'd ask his wife for a divorce. Oh, there had been an exchange of limited promises and some expressions of tenderness that she'd mistaken for love, but what they really wanted from each other was sex, so she figured their relationship probably wouldn't have lasted. Besides, infidelity was very complicated. All that sneaking around made her nervous, and the guilt gave her headaches. It was almost a relief to return to her normal life.

When they met at Burger King for lunch Jenny said, "Wait till you see the suit I found! You're gonna love it. It's just like the one I saw in a magazine. I remember thinking I'd die for a suit like that." She sucked noisily at the suds in the bottom of her glass. "I think I've lost weight since the summer. At least the suit makes me look as if I have, and that's all I care about."

Ellen struggled to appear interested. The mall seemed noisier than ever and the lights were making her dizzy. "So," she said, suddenly wanting to rescue the mood for Jenny's sake. "When am I going to see this fabulous bathing suit?" She hoped she sounded pumped up. If she spoiled the day, it would be just one more count against her in their ongoing skirmish.

They rode an escalator to the second level, where most of the shops that catered to young girls were located. The salesgirl recognized Jenny immediately, and handed her a skimpy, floral-print suit that dangled from its hanger like some limp creature of the sea. "Wait till you see it on, Mom," the salesgirl said, winking at Ellen, who waited outside the partitioned area that served as dressing rooms. Beneath the flimsy curtains, piles of discarded clothing were visible, and when one girl came out wearing a prom dress and hiking boots, everybody laughed.

"Come in here," Jenny finally called. "I can't come out there."

Ellen slid the curtain to one side and stepped inside. It was obvious why Jenny hadn't wanted to model the suit, which was very revealing. "Don't you think it's kind of small?"

"I knew you wouldn't like it. You never like anything I pick out!"

"That's not true, and you know it. It's just that I think you're too young to wear a suit like that. Why not try some other style?"

"They're all like this. Go out and see for yourself. And anyway, I want this one. You said it was my day!"

"That doesn't mean you can buy anything you want to. Not while I'm paying." Suddenly it seemed to Ellen that everyone in the shop had stopped talking and was listening to them.

"I'll never find another suit! And don't tell me I can wear last year's suit, because the chlorine in the fucking club pool fucking ruined it!" She slid to the floor, sobbing.

"Jennifer!" Ellen tried to remember what Karen had been like at fifteen. Jenny, by comparison, seemed so emotional, so out of control. How could anyone get so upset over a bathing suit, Ellen wondered, unless some deeper issue was involved. "Wait a minute. What's this about? It's not about the suit, is it?" She handed Jenny some Kleenex and waited for her to calm down. Much to her relief, the other customers started talking again.

"I'm sick of the way you treat me. When Karen was my age, she was doing whatever she wanted. She was lucky. You sent her away to school."

"You know why we did that. That was the year your father and I split up. Karen was caught in the middle. She wanted to go away. And later, I even asked you if you wanted to go away too, and you said no. You said you'd rather stay home with me. Don't you remember?"

"Well, that was then."

"And now you've changed your mind?"

"Yes. Maybe. I don't know." She lowered her voice to a whisper. "It's getting awful for me at school. It's like I don't have any friends anymore, and the boys think I'm some kind of weirdo because I'm still a virgin." Jenny pulled on her jeans and handed Ellen the suit, which had wet teary splotches down the front.

Ellen sighed. These days everything happened so much earlier. She'd been in college when she'd first had sex, yet here was Jenny, only fifteen, feeling pressure from her peers. Poor little mutt. Suddenly life was so complicated. "Will it really break your heart if you don't get this silly suit?" she asked, thinking Brad would freak out when he saw the way she looked on the beach.

Jenny nodded, and smiled sheepishly. "Pretty dumb, huh?" Jenny hugged her, and Ellen could feel her trembling. Ellen felt a bit shaky herself. Sometimes everything got jumbled between them, and you couldn't tell where one emotion began and another ended.

In another store, Jenny found a cotton strapless sundress and a pair of royal blue canvas sling-backs. "Don't you want to look for anything?" she asked Ellen.

"I bought a warm-up suit for Will."

"God. How can you stand him? He's got hair coming out of his ears. Yech. How can you even let him get near you?"

Ellen felt sorry for Will and for all her other male friends who'd been subjected to Jenny's intense scrutiny since the divorce. Nobody, it seemed, would ever measure up to Brad. Just wait, she thought, until you're stuck with somebody you don't love anymore. She looked at her watch. Perhaps if they left now, they would be home in time to fix an early supper, and she and Will could go to the movies. "Let's call it a day. Okay with you?"

"Sure. I'm cool. Hey, wait. How much money did you say I was getting from Grandma? There's a CD I want to buy, and I just saw it in that window. I'll only be a minute, Mom. Promise. Give me a twenty and I'll pay you back when I cash my birthday check. You sit over there and wait for me." She pointed to a display of patio furniture. Ellen, too tired to resist, plunked herself down in a chaise longue, leaned back, and closed her eyes. She listened to a thrum of voices punctuated by toddlers' cries and boom-box rap. A man passed by and laughed, then asked if she was comfortable enough. A youngster told her not to get sunburned. When she looked at her watch, she realized she'd been there for twenty minutes.

She found Jenny at the back of the music store, leafing through CDs. "I changed my mind. I'm looking for something else, but I don't guess they have it. Why don't we meet in front of Penney's in, like, half an hour?"

∞

"Excuse me," Ellen said to a salesgirl in the sporting goods store. "Could you tell me if the salesman with the beard and the red sweater is still here?" She could feel her heart race. Really, what was she going to say to him? She'd think of something. She just felt she wanted to see him again, if only for a moment, just to confirm she'd done the right thing years before by letting him go.

The girl looked at her with interest. "Something I can do for you?"

Ellen felt her face flush. "No, I . . . that is, I had asked him to hold something for me. A pair of shorts. Look. If he isn't here . . ." Ellen was beginning to feel foolish, although the salesgirl seemed to believe her story.

"Actually, he's gone home for the day. Something about having to take his wife to the doctor. Oh, wait a minute. Maybe he left me a note about the shorts. Lemme go look."

"No, please don't bother," Ellen said quickly. "I, uh, changed my mind about the shorts. Thanks just the same." As she walked quickly out of the store, she imagined what the salesgirl would say about her. *The shoppers you get these days. Go figure!*

Ellen stood outside Penney's and waited for Jenny to return. In one window brightly colored beach towels were suspended by invisible wires against a sky blue–painted backdrop. Plaster gulls held the corners of sheets in their beaks while below, giant plastic shells reposed on a thin layer of bogus sand. For Ellen, the scene recalled a summer of occasional meetings at a small beach house where the mattresses smelled of sea and suntan lotion.

She turned around just in time to see Jenny step off the escalator holding a small bag imprinted with the insignia of the music store. "This is so cool! You and Karen are gonna hate it," Jenny predicted as they exited the mall.

On the way home Jenny was quiet. "Penny for your thoughts," Ellen said finally.

"You really want to know?"

Ellen hesitated before saying yes.

"Okay, then. I'm thinking about all the people in our neighborhood who've gotten divorced."

Caught off guard, Ellen surprised herself by replying casually, "Not that many. Two that I can think of, counting us. The Emersons remarried, so they don't count."

"Sure they do. As far as their kids are concerned, I mean."

"I thought divorce was so commonplace these days that it hardly mattered to anyone."

"What ever gave you a stupid idea like that?"

"I don't know. An article I read. Oprah."

"I know you don't watch Oprah, Mom. And whoever wrote that article is an asshole." Jenny slipped out of her seat belt, slid down in her seat, and hugged herself, propping her knees against the dashboard so that they jiggled with the motion of the car.

Suddenly Ellen was annoyed. "What's with the gloom and doom? Here we've just spent the better part of a day shopping for you, you're going to Bermuda with your dad, your sister's coming home for your birthday . . ."

"Lucky me." Jenny rearranged her body so that she was, once more, belted. "Got anything to chew on?" She reached for Ellen's purse and pawed through the compartments until she found a pack of sugarless gum. "Want some?" Without waiting for an answer she unwrapped a stick, folded it, and reached across to place it in Ellen's mouth. "Look," she said, flinching. "A dead cat. Remember how we put Smitty in the old camp laundry bag and buried her at the back of the property? Daddy had us say a prayer. He said, 'Now let us all give thanks.' Remember? I couldn't figure out what he meant, so I asked you and you said it meant we should remember all the good things about Smitty, that she had been with us for so long and was so affectionate and such a good hunter. I'll always remember because it was around the time you and Daddy started fighting."

Ellen was listening so intently that she almost missed her exit. She swerved abruptly to the right and in doing so cut off the car behind her. The driver honked angrily. "Blow it out your ear!" Jenny yelled. Ellen could feel her heart beating wildly with the realization of their close call. She took a deep breath. When she felt calmer, she asked Jenny, "How did you know? We tried so hard to keep our troubles a secret from you both. We always waited until you went to bed to . . . discuss things."

"Yeah, well, we knew what was going down. We always pretended to be asleep, but we heard everything."

"We never meant for you to be involved," Ellen said weakly, realizing how ridiculous this sounded. She didn't know what else to say, so she kept silent while they passed through a town whose wide main street separated equal rows of century-old houses. At dusk, the lights that shone through the half-drawn shades reminded her of eyes peering out from under heavy lids. Jenny had prodded her memory. She recalled a particular evening when she and Brad had driven to their therapist's office, which was located in this town. It was a rainy evening early in October, and fallen leaves stuck to the wet pavement like blobs of color on an artist's palette. She and Brad wore jeans, heavy sweaters, and trench coats: two people dressed alike, giving an impression of synchrony.

Jenny reached over and touched her mother's arm gently. "I didn't mean to upset you. I only wanted to ask you something. Do you ever wish you and Daddy had stayed together?"

Ellen felt her throat tighten. "I guess I feel there isn't a simple answer to the question. Do you understand?"

"Yeah. Sort of. You're not mad because I asked, are you?"

"Of course not." Actually she felt relieved, as though the air had been cleared between them. Now she could turn her complete attention to the road ahead, which twisted as it rose to a much higher elevation. They were approaching a rest area that had a view of the entire valley. It was a place she had come with her lover years ago. She remembered feeling free then, but only for a short time; this she remembered as she guided the car up the steep hill into the soft spring night.

FEAR OF FALLING

Doyle sits at the breakfast table, watches dust particles jump in the morning light, and admires his wife, Helen, whose skin is fair and smooth as a young girl's. Her light brown hair, flecked with gray, falls straight to her shoulders, then curls up slightly to fit the clavicular dip. She wears her bangs long so that they skim her thick eyebrows. He's decided she's perfect in every respect save one: She smokes. "I'll get fat if I quit," she tells him. "You don't want me fat, do you?" Doyle notices how adorably round her small feet look in the puffy slippers he gave her for Christmas. "Well," Helen says in a voice thick with early-morning huskiness, "are we going or aren't we?"

He focuses on his right leg, encased in a full cast. He has propped it up on a folding canvas stool that he takes from room to room, from their house to his office, which is in a converted barn located a few steps from their back door. The only other psychiatrist in the area has his office in the multi-specialty clinic downtown, but Doyle has always considered this placement a boon to patients who wish to protect their privacy. In another two weeks the cast will be shortened, his orthopedist has promised. It's been only a month since he fractured his ankle and tore some ligaments, but it seems like a year.

"I don't mind driving," Helen continues. "It'd be a shame to miss all the colors. In another week the trees'll be bare. You always love to see the last hurrah." She reaches across the table and touches his hand. "We can take a picnic, some fruit, a bottle of wine. Maybe we can even stop at an orchard and pick some apples. You could sit in a lawn chair with your foot propped up while Susie and I pick."

Doyle sighs, resisting. While it's true he loves to see the last of the foliage, his discomfort riding in the car is considerable, because if his leg is down for a long time it begins to throb.

Helen anticipates him. "You can sit in the backseat with your leg up if you like," she says. "Please, baby. I think you need an outing. I think we need one, too."

He lifts his leg cautiously, bends down to fold the stool, which he props against the table leg, and stands up. The top of the cast cuts into the flesh of his thigh and he winces. "I can't stand being hauled around like an invalid."

"But you are an invalid—at least temporarily—and I don't mind hauling you around."

"All right," Doyle says curtly. "We'll go. I'll sit in the front seat, though. And I'll stand while you pick apples. I refuse to sit in a lawn chair like that old fart who hands out bags."

Helen laughs. "If we bring the portable radio, you could pass for his son. You could collect the money and nobody would ever know. The son even has a limp. With your pants covering your cast, who'd ever know?"

"That's not funny," he says, and means it. There are times he hates her sense of humor.

At that moment, their daughter Susie enters the room and breaks the tension. She's come from the shower wearing her brother's old bathrobe, and her long wet hair clings to her head like the sleek fur of an aquatic mammal. "Who would never know what?" she asks.

"Your mother has a perverse sense of humor these days," Doyle grouses.

Helen adds, "It's a private joke."

Susie shrugs her shoulders and forages around the kitchen for some food. "Doughnuts. All *right!*"

"I'm going to crawl upstairs and get dressed. We should probably leave by ten if we're going to stop and pick apples." Doyle looks at Susie to see if she's pleased. When she smiles, powdered sugar clings to the corners of her mouth. He bends forward to kiss the top of her head and inhales the perfume of her shampoo, a sweet floral scent that reminds him of summer.

Now Helen stands at the counter making sandwiches for their picnic. "There's a jar of pickles in the refrigerator," she tells Doyle. "Will you put it in the cooler? And make sure Susie got the Riesling from the back room. We're saving the Beaujolais for Thanksgiving. You said you wanted roast beef instead of turkey, remember?"

"We hardly ever have beef," he says defensively. "Besides, it's Bill's favorite. Speaking of which, I hope to God he doesn't bring home another refugee from the homeless shelter. The last one smelled like overripe garbage and his nose ran all the time. I don't see how coddling junkies is going to enhance his stint as a seminarian." Bill is studying to be an Episcopal priest, a vocation that strikes Doyle as foreign and foreboding.

Cradling the pickles in his right arm, he tucks his crutches in his armpits and slowly makes his way to the back door, feeling like a piece of rusting machinery. He is terrified by stairs; one lurch in the wrong direction and he could go hurtling down. There are only three steps here, and he takes them cautiously. A few more feet and he'll be outside the pen where Susie's probably feeding the pups, her hands flashing from one small wriggling animal to another, soothing, patting. She's always been crazy about animals.

When she turns to face him, he can see that her jeans are coated with hair, the mother's postpartum sheddings. The pups hunker back and pull at Susie's pants with razor-sharp teeth the size of corn kernels. "The runt is walking well now," she says, her eyes shining. "We don't have to do anything about him, do we?"

"No, baby." He lies. The vet has examined the pup and suspects a heart defect. Doyle was supposed to arrange a disposal, but his injury interfered; now he's glad he didn't get around to it. This way the pup will die when his time is up, like most other creatures. "Hey, Suze," he says, grabbing her hand and almost losing his balance. "Help your gimpy old dad out to the car, will you?"

It's eleven when they finally get started. Doyle has been the one to hold things up. At the last minute, he makes Susie check their answering machine. There is one message from a long-term patient, one of the few to whom he has given their unlisted number.

"What did she say?" he wants to know.

" 'I know it's your day off, but please call me.' Something like that. She didn't sound real worried, if that's what you need to know."

Doyle hesitates, aware there's always the chance that Marjorie, the patient, is in desperate need. Yet how many times has he responded promptly, only to get a busy signal or no answer at all? No, he won't rise to the bait this time, he decides. He'll call back when they return from their day's outing.

Once, when Doyle was out of town, Helen helped Marjorie weather a minor crisis; a boyfriend had neglected to call her on her birthday. "The woman was a basket case," Helen said. "I tried to calm her down, but nothing seemed to work. Finally I just told her what I thought made sense. I told her to get a good night's rest. Things almost always look better in the morning, I said. Maybe the jerk would realize his mistake and call the next day. She seemed to like that possibility, and finally hung up."

Weeks later, Helen told Doyle she'd seen Marjorie at the supermarket. "I caught this ordinary-looking, middle-aged woman staring at me across the frozen food bins. Then, when she spoke to the checkout clerk, I recognized her voice. I almost said something to her, but I thought you might not approve."

"What made you think that?"

"Oh, I don't know. I guess I thought I might be breaking some sort of taboo. You know, doctor's wife tries to interfere in therapeutic relationship. That sort of thing."

Doyle chuckled. "She'd probably have kept you there an hour."

"Maybe that was what stopped me. There was a long line at the checkout, and I didn't want to hold people up."

"You should do whatever makes you feel comfortable," he said, responding in knee-jerk fashion, as he often did with patients. "Of course, she's harmless. Mostly lonely. She'd have probably loved it if you'd struck up a conversation." He thought of all the times he'd had to talk Marjorie off the phone or out of his office. *But the fifty minutes can't be up, your clock must be wrong, there's nobody in the waiting room so I don't see why you can't let me stay longer, is it the money? You know I can afford to pay you, so why don't you give me a break?* Poor desperate creature, starved for attention. "But I can appreciate your reluctance to jump in cold," he added, wanting to assure Helen she'd done the right thing.

"Well," Helen continued, "I felt comfortable getting the hell out of there. I don't know why, really. Maybe I was afraid she'd make a scene."

"She's not really a scene-maker."

"Now you're making me feel guilty."

Doyle smiled. He touched his wife's cheek. She was so kind, so tolerant of others' idiosyncrasies, so much so that he sometimes thought she should have been the therapist.

At the orchard gate, an old man with puckered brown skin is handing out worn paper shopping bags and long poles with canvas sacks at the end. "Take this'n," he says to Susie and winks at her. Suddenly Doyle notices how her shirt gaps between buttons and pulls across her breasts. No wonder the old goat is turned on.

"Rob, you'd better stay here until we find you a level spot for resting," Helen says, looking ahead to a congested path that snakes down a small hill into the trees. Beside them on the road, cars are parked bumper to bumper, some wedged in tightly, some tilting crazily on the embankment. Families carrying baskets and bags of apples teeter toward them. The old geezer collects money, making change from a tin box that rests on the ground next to his transistor radio. Rock music surfaces above static. "Where's your chair?" Helen asks. "I know I put it in the trunk."

"I took it out because I didn't want to bring it," he says, anticipating the annoyance his reply will produce, but Helen just shrugs and puts up her hands, as if to say, *I give up.* "Why don't you two go on ahead? I'll follow at my own speed," he suggests curtly. They've been coming here so many years that Doyle has memorized the layout. He knows which varieties grow where and which sections are more inclined to be picked out first. "We can meet at the second gate, just before the Cortlands." He watches Helen and Susie as they trot ahead, swinging their empty bags, giggling like schoolgirls.

The uneven ground makes using crutches more difficult than ever, and soon he's forced to rest, which affords him an opportunity to observe the sun-drenched fruit that hangs from the trees beneath a pristine sky. Around him apples thunk to the ground, displaced by children who scamper in the trees like monkeys. The most agile climbers straddle the thinner branches near the top and dislodge the fruit by wiggling their bodies. Helen and Susie are way ahead now, but he doesn't care; he's having too much fun. A young woman lopes by, a sleeping baby strapped to her chest. Doyle is moved to tears by the woman's easy grace. Pinching the crutch pads under his arms and leaning forward slightly for balance, he wipes his eyes with his knuckles. *Mustn't let them see me blubbering like an old fool.*

Helen was right about the chair, which would have enabled him to stay on the sidelines and read in comfort rather than suffer with a leg that throbbed with every wobbly step. Just as he is about to collapse on the ground in a despairing heap, he sees Helen's red pullover and Susie, with her dark green sweatshirt tied around her waist. They have a bag of apples between them and another in their outside hands. "Here, let me," he yells, then realizes how silly he sounds. How can he help with anything?

To picnic, they settle on the state park where, in past winters, they've skied. The year Bill was on the racing team, they followed him from meet to meet, standing dutifully with the other parents, freezing and cheering and sharing the relief when the season ended and they could once more spend quiet weekends at home. Doyle was always grateful that Susie skied just for the fun of it. If she'd been a racer, he would have worried about injury. Not that he hadn't worried about Bill, but Susie was delicate (or he thought of her as such). As a family, they'd been enormously lucky. Helen once sprained her wrist falling on the north face, but that had been the only skiing mishap. When Bill was an undergraduate, he'd pulled a ligament scaling cliffs with Outward Bound. Doyle shuddered to think what else could have happened on that adventure. As for his own injury, it occurred while hiking on a gentle slope just a hundred yards from the base camp. Noticing the trail was slick from heavy rains, he'd turned to warn Helen, "Watch your step," as he felt his leg give way.

As they pull into the parking area, Susie spots a picnic table at the base of the novice slope where she learned to ski. They park, and Helen gets out of the car to open the trunk. "You stay put," she orders Doyle. "We'll carry the stuff over and then we'll come back for you."

"I'm okay," he insists. "I made it into the orchard and back, didn't I?"

"But this is uphill."

"I can do it. If I have to, I'll lean on old Suze here." He grimaces as he stands up, then proceeds slowly in the direction of the picnic site. He can feel his heart slamming in his chest as it had when he exerted himself in the orchard. "I'm too fucking fat," he mutters. "When I get out of this cast, I'm going on a diet and working out at the gym." Helen has religion about her diet and the NordicTrack, which she uses twenty minutes a day, twice a day, to keep herself thin and trim. He looks down and bemoans his flabby gut. How could he have let himself go like this? And his hair is thinning. When he looked into the mirror this morning, he could see more of his scalp than he'd ever seen before. Christ! Why was it so hard to get old? Even now, on this outing, which is supposed to cheer him up, he can feel himself tipping over into sadness. His therapist's acumen assures him this isn't a significant slide into depression, but rather just a dip into melancholy that's taking the edge off even the keenest pleasures, like the smell of Helen's hair as she slips into bed beside him each night.

He watches her now as she lugs picnic paraphernalia. The sun is making her squint, but even when she squints she's beautiful. Her face shines when she smiles. Susie whispers something to her and as she rolls her head back to laugh, her large breasts jiggle beneath her sweater. Doyle knows she isn't wearing a bra. Just the thought of this usually weakens him with desire, but now he waits in vain for his body to respond to a sexy daydream. In anger, he plants his crutches carelessly on the uneven ground and almost falls.

"Wine?" He nods his head as she uncorks the bottle and proceeds to fill the cup he holds in an outstretched, shaky hand. "You okay?"

"Just got a little scared, is all. I almost fell down back there." Sitting on the picnic bench, he realizes how lucky he is to have made it up the hill.

"You shouldn't take chances."

"And you shouldn't worry."

"I won't if you won't."

"What's that supposed to mean?"

"Just what I said."

"What makes you think I'm worried?"

"Your eyes, Robert. I can always tell how you're feeling by the expression in your eyes."

She rarely calls him by his full name. Usually it's Rob. Never Bob, and especially not Bobby, the diminutive his mother uses. "I have no secrets from you, then? Not even when I'm wearing these?" He removes his dark glasses and makes a face at her, feigning annoyance. "Is there no place I can hide?"

"What're you two babbling about? Let's eat." Susie digs into the cooler and pulls out sandwiches and a container of deviled eggs. "Cholesterol is bad for you," she teases Doyle, "so I'll eat yours."

She unfolds a small triangle of waxed paper and sprinkles salt on an egg. "And salt is bad for you, so you shouldn't have any of that, either." She pilfers her father's wine and takes a generous swig. "And too much of this is *very* bad for you, so I'll have to help you drink it!"

"Very funny," Doyle says, grabbing the bottle and almost dropping it in the process. "Suddenly she's a comedian. Are you catching her act, Helen?"

"Remember when we used to come here every week with the ski team?" Helen asks, ignoring the banter. "Bill used to love it so."

"Yeah. Now he never skis," Doyle remarks sadly, replenishing his wine. "It's too expensive. He's taken a vow of poverty, y'know."

"That's a stupid thing to say, Daddy. You know how he feels about asking you for money. He says it's costing you enough to send him through school."

"It isn't about money, any of it," Helen says. "He's dedicating his life to others. I think it's wonderful."

"It isn't as if he's going to be a monk," Susie adds. "In the Episcopal Church, ministers can marry, so he's not going to be some weenie-wagging weirdo."

Doyle tilts back his head and drains his wine. "Do tell."

Helen begins to clear the table. "If Bill were here, he'd be telling me to recycle everything."

"Mm. Garbage collectors—pardon me, used-food engineers—will be out of work if Bill has his way." Doyle stands up and reaches forward, gathering paper plates and napkins. "He'd be horrified if he saw they have only one trash barrel here." He has a wine buzz, just enough to take the edge off his discomfort but make him feisty at the same time. As he lurches toward the trash barrel, he bangs the side of his cast against a table leg. "Goddamned nuisance," he mutters, wondering why he should feel tipsy after two cups of wine. Then he remembers the antidepressant he'd taken before leaving the house. Had he checked the dose? Christ, he was getting careless.

In the bathroom, the water he drinks from his cupped hands tastes of copper, and when he straightens up, he begins to feel dizzy. "Mustn't alarm them," he says out loud. He urinates, trapping the crutches in his armpits so they won't fall. "There, that's better," he says with a sigh, grateful that part of his anatomy is cooperating.

The water has left an unpleasant metallic taste in his mouth, but the vertigo has gone.

He lingers at the sink, wanting to postpone the trek back to the picnic table, but he knows if he waits too long they'll come after him, so he thuds outside into the afternoon glare.

"There you are," Helen says brightly. "How about riding the gondola? I'll bring the car up close so we can drive over. The view from the top is splendid, remember?"

Just the thought of looking down from the cable car is enough to make Doyle feel queasy. "I don't think so," he says. "You and Susie go. I'll stay here and take a nap." He can feel tears of self-denial welling up, a return of the sadness that continues to wash over him from time to time. He thinks of the beach they frequent in Maine and wishes it were as easy to predict the ebb and flow of his emotional tide.

"All right, if you're sure you won't get weepy without us here to cheer you up."

"I won't," he lies. The tide is rolling in, and he wants them to go before he's engulfed. "Go. I'll be fine. Enjoy the view." He turns away, deflecting Helen's kiss. In a matter of seconds Susie will see him reduced to the level of a blubbering child. He hobbles away from them and spreads the red-checkered picnic cloth on the ground beneath some pine trees. Using his rolled-up jacket as a pillow, he prepares to lie down, figuring that sleep, if it comes, will provide a welcome, if temporary, escape from his self-induced misery.

Doyle wakes to sounds of shouting. Nearby, a group of youngsters is doing calisthenics. He guesses they are members of the same team Bill used to work out with one day a week. The youngsters, boys and girls of varied ages, run up the beginner's slope, pause at the crest of the hill, and, on command from their coach, begin their descent planting their poles at the tops of imaginary moguls. At the bottom of the hill they fall down, exhausted, and the scene resembles a blissfully benign battlefield. The respite is cut short by an abrupt command, and the group breaks into two lines for a relay race. They move easily through a variety of conditioning exercises that make Doyle wince: frog leaps, duck and crab walks, backward and forward rolls. One boy has to be coaxed repeatedly to the finish line. Doyle understands. He remembers that Bill always hated training. Helen had been the one to push; his conscience is clear on that score.

Suddenly the youngsters are climbing into a bus, and he is left alone to wonder why it's taking so long for Helen and Susie to admire the view. He'd counted on being home before dark. Marjorie will have been trying to reach him all day. Seized with apprehension, he recalls a half-hearted suicide attempt, something to do with pills. Why hadn't he thought to bring the cell phone?

Just when he's letting himself in for some serious castigation, Susie bounces up the hill and dispels the gloom. "You should have come, Daddy. It was awesome! We walked all around the summit. You could've sat in the restaurant and had coffee."

Helen administers a therapeutic hug. "Look at you, Rob. You're shivering, you poor baby."

He pities Marjorie, with no one to offer her comfort.

They've put him in the back of the car so he can elevate his leg. He sleeps off and on, waking to the women's soft babble. They're talking about some friend of Bill's who's gone to live in Boston. Susie wishes she could live there when she's older. Helen points out the disadvantages of living in a big city. Doyle consoles himself that Susie, being predictable, will not bolt from the nest before it's time for her to leave. Bill is the one who's full of surprises.

Helen is smoking. He can feel his mucous membranes reacting, and any minute now he'll start to cough. Too many of his female patients smoke. Although he disapproves, he admits there's something seductive about an attractive woman with a cigarette in her mouth. *How transparent is that?* he thinks, remembering that he likes the aroma of Marjorie's brand, which takes him back to med school when he was smoking a pack and a half a day. At this moment, sitting in the backseat of their car nursing a bum leg, he'd give anything for a smoke, even one of Helen's Virginia Slims. He tries closing his eyes and breathing deeply, a meditative technique he's learned from Bill. It doesn't work. When he opens his eyes, he still wants a cigarette.

He fishes for the small bottle of pills he keeps in his pocket and wonders if he dares to swallow one without water. Anxiety overwhelms him. He feels if he can't have a pill, something terrible will happen. The symptoms, which patients have described in desperate attempts to get him to write prescriptions, are all too familiar. He never lets them off the hook easily, preferring to emphasize the need to understand one's anxieties rather than mask them with drugs. No pusher of Prozac he. The week before, when he consulted a colleague, the man attempted to reassure him: "No wonder you feel bad. You've never been ill. Now you feel totally helpless and vulnerable. You're a temporary invalid. Let's emphasize *temporary.* Soon you'll be back to normal, maybe even in time to ski. So go home and have a drink with that gorgeous wife of yours and forget about your troubles," he said, writing Doyle a prescription.

Helen navigates the sharp turn that leads to their road. "Almost home," she says to him. "Did you have a good nap?"

"Yes." He yawns convincingly.

"You're going to let Susie and me take everything in from the car, Robert. Understand?"

"Yes," he murmurs, docile as an obedient child. At the same time, he feels useless and sad. He's afraid he'll start to cry. *Please dear God if there is a God don't let me cry.* The road narrows into a path that marks the approach to their property. Helen's window is open slightly, enough to let in the early-evening sounds, the flutter of wings and the click of dry branches. In the distance a barred owl hoots. In another moment the house will be visible, rising against the sky like a beached ship. Land's End, they've named it. Some friends consider the setting desolate. Some patients object to the road, which is poorly maintained in winter. Most, however, welcome the privacy. "I've got to make a phone call," Doyle says suddenly. "I think I'll do it from the office. Would you mind letting me off here?"

"Want me to come with you?" Susie offers. "I promise I won't eavesdrop."

"Thanks, no." He struggles to get out of the car. Helen has stopped at the end of the stone walk that leads directly to the patients' entrance. "Just shine the flashlight at the door until I get there, okay?" Doyle watches his shadow bounce against the side of the building. His hands are shaking as he takes the key from its hiding place and fits it into the lock. Inside and slightly to the left is a switch that will flood the small waiting room with light. Blinking in the brightness, he removes his jacket and drapes it over a chair before making his way slowly to his desk. As he eases into his swivel chair, the crutches thud to the floor.

He picks up the receiver and dials Marjorie's number from memory, then waits impatiently for her to answer. He knows she's home. When she's agitated she always waits at home for him to get back to her, to soothe her and reassure her that she can continue to balance on the tightrope of her life, even though she's convinced she'll fall. "We're all afraid of falling," he remembers telling her on more than one occasion.

A soft and tentative voice says "Hello?" and then sighs.

He shivers at the dramatic intensity of the sound. As he listens to her catalog the day's despair, he recognizes his own inability to cope with the blows that have recently been dealt him. For a moment, he's startled to feel an affinity with this miserable creature who goes around and around and gets nowhere. He thinks of all the times he's wanted to take her by the shoulders, shake her, and say, "You. You can stop what's happening to you. Only you." Now, miraculously, he feels himself beginning to relax for the first time in weeks. Although he recognizes the danger in Marjorie's manipulative behavior, it pleases him to know that she depends on him. As she bores him with the minute details of her pitiful life, he gains strength. He nods in agreement: *Yes, I know how that feels, I've been there too.*

At the same time, he focuses on the second shelf of a corner bookcase where Susie's fourth-grade Christmas gift sits, a piece of driftwood with shells glued onto it, souvenir of a trip to Cape Cod. Next to it sits a framed photograph of the four of them, a candid shot taken in the White Mountains by a fellow hiker. Susie is the only one not smiling. Doyle remembers taking her to the orthodontist the day before to have her braces fitted. The shelf above holds Bill's slalom trophies from prep school. "You keep these, Dad," he'd said when he went off to college.

Doyle's forgotten how much he loves this room.

Now his leg is acting up again. He feels the burden of fatigue, and wishes Marjorie would get on with it so he could go back to the house and enjoy a nightcap. The receiver is moist in his grip. He toys with the idea of telling her he has to handle an emergency at the hospital just to get her off the phone, but he can't lie. "Do you feel I should, then?" she asks at the end of a long harangue having to do with her sister.

"If it feels comfortable, yes, you should," he says, hoping this will be the end of it, at least for the time being.

"Well, then. I will." Her voice sounds stronger. "Tuesday?"

"Yes. Three-thirty, as always." He waits for her to hang up before releasing a pent-up sigh. Poor Marjorie, he thinks. There will never be enough Tuesdays.

Later, when the warmth of Drambuie has turned him supple and mellow, he makes the cumbersome journey up the stairs to their bedroom and undresses by moonlight. Helen sleeps on her right side with her left arm flung over his pillow. He moves her arm gently and rolls into bed beside her. The delicate fragrance of bath oil that leaves a sheen on her skin arouses him, and he moves closer to caress her breasts. The cast makes intimacy difficult, but there are ways. "Helen," he whispers. When she turns to face him, her eyes are open and she is smiling.

DELPHINIUMS BLUE

Carol notices that the kitchen faucet needs a new washer and wonders if her daughter's boyfriend, Tim, knows more about plumbing than he does about gardening. "Let me help you with the gardening," he had said the day before. "I know what to do. Didn't Audrey tell you I used to work summers for a landscaping firm?"

Before she could stop him, he was digging up the large delphinium bed outside her bedroom window, the one her husband, Howard, had put in years before. "Hey, wait a minute," she yelled, but it was already too late; the limp plants lay in heaps beside the upturned earth like strange creatures from the sea, and all she could do was wring her hands in desperation.

She stood beside him and they both surveyed the damage. "You'll be much happier with irises," he said with authority. "Delphiniums should never be left by themselves."

"But they weren't left by themselves. Howard always planted red geraniums in this bed! Oh damn it, never mind," she muttered angrily. "You wouldn't understand."

"Jesus, Mrs. McMartin, I'm sorry," he said, picking up one of the plants and examining it. "Maybe I can replant them," he added lamely, "although some are starting to bloom and you're not supposed to be able to move them while they're blooming." He put down the plants gently on the ground, stood up, and shifted his feet. "Does that sound right to you?"

"You're supposed to be the expert."

"Look, I really thought you'd like irises better. I never meant to upset you like this."

She saw him in a different light then, sensing his discomfort, and tried to cover her disappointment by putting him at ease. "I suppose you think I'm a fool for being so sentimental, especially after what's happened between Howard and me," she said.

He didn't reply. Instead, he took the pile of limp delphiniums off to the compost heap and did his best to make the bed look presentable by raking the soil and covering up the wounds left by the uprooted plants.

Later, when he asked her for the keys to her car so he could go pick up iris rhizomes and fertilizer, she watched him drive away, hoping he wouldn't floor the accelerator all the way into town. She was beginning to regret her decision to let him stay with her. When they returned from seeing Audrey off to California, he said it would be only a couple of days, just until he could line up a summer job on the Cape. It had already been a week.

That night as she lay in the big bed she'd shared with Howard for so many years, she remembered the afternoon he'd planted the delphiniums. It was shortly after they had purchased the house, during Audrey's infancy. "What queer little plants," she'd said when she first saw them. "Don't tell me they're going to end up looking pretty."

"They have these long spikes that bloom," he'd said. "Just wait till you see."

She'd watched while he planted red geraniums throughout, alternating them with the delphiniums in an orderly fashion, before asking, "Why geraniums?"

"Don't you remember A. A. Milne's poem about the dormouse? 'And all the day long he'd a wonderful view / Of geraniums (red) and delphiniums (blue).' Hey. Come here, you," he'd said, standing up and turning to face her. He'd wiped the soil from his hands by brushing his palms on the seat of his pants, and they'd made love in the early afternoon while Audrey slept upstairs in a small room where violets danced over the walls against a background of yellowed paper.

At dinner Carol says, "You must miss Audrey a great deal," and reaches across the table to touch Tim's hand.

"Yes," he admits. "But I'm not sure she misses me."

"Oh, I'm sure she does."

"Then why doesn't she write?"

"Audrey's never been a writer," Carol says. "At least she's never written me more than the required number of letters when she's been away from home. You know, the kind of letters that say, 'I'm okay, Mom, don't worry about me.' "

"She's always written when we've been apart. That's what worries me now."

"Oh, you know her friend Marion. Always on the go. I bet Audrey's just caught up in that." She pauses, wondering what to say next. "*El Norte*'s in town, that movie about the Guatemalan immigrants. It's supposed to be terrific. Want to go see it?" Suddenly she wants to do anything she can to lift his spirits, to make him happy again.

"I don't really feel like seeing a movie," he says dully, picking at the remains of his dinner. "But if you want to go for a swim . . ."

She hesitates, remembering the stares of curious onlookers two days before, when she'd taken Tim to the country club for lunch. "This is my daughter's fiancé," she'd told them, while resenting the need to explain. *What do I care what they think? If they want to fabricate some silly rumor, let them.* "A swim would be nice." *Let them think whatever they want.*

In her room, Carol selects the one-piece suit she ordered from a catalog, a snug-fitting tank with high-cut legs that flatters her too-soft body, and pulls on the sweatpants she appropriated from Audrey's closet, pleased she can wear her daughter's loose-fitting workout wardrobe despite their difference in size. Audrey retains her perfect size 6 figure, her reward for going to the gym on a regular basis and watching her diet, while Carol, not looking to please men, has given up her exercise regimen and eats anything she wants. Now, as she looks at herself in the mirror, she regrets her indifference. *How did my upper arms get so flabby? Is that a double chin?* Disappointed, she selects a long-sleeved turtleneck jersey, too warm for this time of year, and slips it over her head. At least the color is becoming, she decides. *And anyway, why should I care what Tim thinks?*

They park her car in the lot beside the clubhouse and walk out to sit on the large flat rocks that lead down to the water. "Do you know the people in this club very well?" Tim asks.

Carol notices his bony knees with their shiny, stretched-out skin and thinks of Audrey doing yoga on the living room rug. "I've known them for years, but they're not close friends, if that's what you're asking. Most of them are married to Howard's former golfing buddies."

"Those women are stuffy old bags compared to you. You seem so much younger."

"Well, thanks for the compliment, but actually, we're all about the same age."

Tim turns to look at her. "And what age is that?" he asks dryly.

Carol avoids his eyes. Instead, she focuses on the weathered dock, where someone, probably a lovesick teenager, close in age to this boy who is making her feel uncomfortable, has scratched the name of his beloved with a penknife. "Most women I know prefer to keep their age a secret," she murmurs primly, thinking, *What difference would it make if I told him?* and feeling ashamed by her reluctance to do so. "If we're going to swim, we'd better do it now," she says abruptly. "It'll be dusk in half an hour. You can't see the rocks as well then, and you can get a nasty cut if you aren't careful."

He startles her by grabbing her wrists. "I'll race you to the point!" he says loudly, pulling Carol to her feet.

She's surprised by his strength until she remembers that Audrey had told her he lifts weights. Above them and to the left, Howard's pals stand chatting and drinking on the clubhouse veranda, their wives clustered in the corner within easy eyeshot of the dock.

"Don't tell me you're worried about what *they* think," he says, picking up on her concern. "They probably gossip about everybody." He lets her hands drop and guides her to the edge of the dock. "Let's show those nosy bitches what a good swimmer you are!"

Before she can worry about how cold the water is, they're swimming toward the marker, their strokes almost in synchrony, and she can feel her heart beating from excitement and exertion. It's been years since she's been challenged to a race. Now she thinks her heart will explode, but just when she thinks she'll have to drop back, they reach the buoy.

He lets her touch it first. "There you are," he says. "You won!"

Breathless, she can only force a smile.

"You're some awesome swimmer," he says appreciatively. "We can take it easy going back, if you like."

Bristling at this suggestion, yet still struggling for breath, she insists, "I feel fine!"

As she pushes off into the dark water she wonders why she hasn't thought of swimming more often, since it makes her feel so strong and good.

Back at the house, she lets him shower first. Her swimmer's high is beginning to wear off, and she's left with some feelings she doesn't totally understand. On the ride back from the club Tim was quiet. At first she assumed he was annoyed at losing the race back to shore (a legitimate loss that sent her head reeling), but there was something else in his attitude that puzzled her. She wonders if he has a crush on her. Not that she considers herself the type of woman who would attract a younger man, but he might, in his disappointment over

Audrey, turn to her for comfort. In his state he could easily mistake a need to be consoled for physical attraction.

"All done!" he shouts to her from the bathroom. "If you hurry, we can catch the nine o'clock show."

She waits until he goes back upstairs, then yells, "I thought you didn't want to go to the movies."

"I changed my mind." When he comes down to the landing beside her, he's wearing his undershorts and toweling his hair. "You seemed so hot to see *El Norte*. I guess I figured it must be a really good film."

His boxer shorts are shredded at the hems. This, and the fact that his uncombed, still-wet hair is sticking straight up, makes him seem vulnerable to her. "Well, I've changed my mind," she says curtly, thinking, *He's got a nerve standing there in his underpants. Who does he think I am, his mother?* When she notices his hurt expression, she softens. "I think I overdid the swimming. After all, I'm not as young as I used to be."

"Come on, Carol! That doesn't sound natural, coming from you," he says, using her given name for the first time.

She's close enough to touch him, but keeps her arms at her sides. "How would you know what's natural for me?" she asks, trying to keep her voice even. "We hardly know each other. Audrey's the one you know, remember? Look, uh, I think it's time for you to be moving on, Tim. I'll drive you to town first thing tomorrow morning. There's an early bus to Boston. You'd better get your things together tonight."

For several minutes he's silent. Then he yells, "What the fuck did I do wrong this time?" When she doesn't answer, he runs upstairs to Audrey's room and slams the door.

Later that evening, after she has readied herself for bed, Carol walks over to the large window that overlooks the garden and watches the June bugs slam against the back-door screen. Moths circle the lantern that sheds light on what had been her favorite part of the backyard. She thinks about the dormouse who'd been happy in his flower bed until the well-meaning doctor prescribed a change of scene. The dormouse's salvation had been his ability to shut his eyes and pretend he was back in his old surroundings. *Is that what I've been trying to do ever since Howard left?*

In the middle of the night she wakes to sounds in the backyard but, convinced the noises are made by raccoons raiding the garbage she soon falls back asleep.

She gets up at six the next morning and takes her first cup of coffee out on the patio, where she notices something different about the flower beds beneath her bedroom window—where there were irises, there are now delphiniums and geraniums, their small leaves glistening with tiny drops of dew. She kneels on the wet ground to touch them. All around her the first marvels of the day manifest themselves: silvery spiders' webs, hovering bees, robins out to pluck worms from the spongy soil. She becomes so absorbed in her surroundings that at first she doesn't notice Tim, who has walked quietly out of the house.

"You did this?"she asks, tears spilling onto her cheeks. "Why?"

"I wanted to make things right before I left."

"Have you had breakfast? There's coffee if you want some, and muffins."

"I'm not hungry. When does the bus leave?" His voice is dull. He shoves his hands in his pockets and rocks back on his heels, reminding her of Audrey in one of her pouts. She thinks he looks younger than he did the first time she met him, the Thanksgiving that Audrey brought him home and announced proudly, "Mom, Dad, this is Tim."

"Seven-thirty. We don't have much time, do we? I'd better get dressed," she says.

He sits quietly beside her in the front seat of the station wagon.

"Let me know how everything turns out," Carol says. "I hope

you find a job you'll like for the rest of the summer. And in September . . ."

"I'm not going back to school in the fall. I think I'll work for a while."

"Landscaping?"

He laughs. "No, I don't think so. I'm giving up gardening."

"A wise decision," she says, laughing also. "Although I did like what you came up with the second time. Howard, damn him, would have been delighted."

"Speaking of Mr. McMartin, I'll make a bet you and he work things out. I know Audrey wishes you would." He pauses, leans back, and puts his left arm up across the back of the seat, almost touching her hair with his hand. "And you, Mrs. McMartin. What do you wish?"

Carol thinks for a minute. "I'm not sure," she says slowly. "I know that if he did come back, things would never be the same. But maybe that would be good." She turns into a parking space next to the bus station. "Oh, what does it matter, anyhow? Howard will do his thing, and I'll do mine, and if we end up doing it together, well . . ."

Tim gets out of the car, opens the back door, and pulls out his duffel bag. "How tentative," he says. "And how weird."

"That's how life is when you're middle-aged. Tentative and weird."

When the bus arrives, he says, "I'm not sure how to say goodbye."

Impulsively, she kisses him lightly on the lips, but when he tries to return her kiss, she moves away. "I hope things turn out well for you," she says. She watches him board the bus and choose a window on her side. He presses his face against the pane and mouths some words; she shakes her head to show she doesn't understand. Then, as the bus pulls away, she thinks how easy it would have been to ask him to stay, how easy in the most complicated sort of way.

KEEPSAKE

"I'm in Columbus to visit my mother and sister," I say as I step off the 737. Who knows what prompts this confession? Landing jitters, followed by a sense of relief at having made it safely to the ground once more? By the time I've said my little piece, the smiling flight attendant is half a terminal away.

Six months have passed since I entrusted my mother to my younger sister Trish's care, the longest stretch I've ever gone without hearing, "Oh. You've done something different with your hair." Just before she left for Ohio, Mom and I had a fight, one of many concerning Pop's treatment of Trish. Mom never remembers events, not to mention hairstyles, the way I do. "Don't speak ill of the dead," she scolded. "Of course I know you never really loved him. You don't even love *me*." What's love got to do with perfect recall? I wondered.

"Look at it this way," friends console. "She's Trish's problem now."

My sister was once voted the prettiest girl in all Rhode Island. She won that title in a beauty contest when she was sixteen, the summer we waitressed together. In our off-hours, we'd lie on the roof of our boardinghouse and soak up the rays, glistening in our sheen of baby oil, faces framed in the triangles of homemade foil reflectors. While Trish bronzed, my tender Phisohexed skin, spandexed into submission, raged against the noonday sun. A skimpy bikini hid Trish's perfectly molded tits and ass, but her one flaw, a puffy welt of scar tissue below her left buttock, remained in tantalizing view. *Don't.* I can see Pop's right hand raised, his leather belt with the heavy metal buckle trailing down his arm. *Don't.*

One afternoon that summer, we picked up two good-looking, fast-talking punks who promised to show us a good time. They took us to a bar, where we ordered Seagram's and Seven. Trish danced solo to the jukebox, her small breasts jiggling crazily to Bill Haley and the Comets. When I told them how old she was, they dumped us both. Trish was rumpled from necking in the backseat, but she was still gorgeous. That summer when we doubled, I knew I was just along for the ride. I also knew I had to be there, to save my sister from herself.

She's waiting for me at the gate, a standout in her long red coat with its perky black velvet collar and cuffs to match, her lightened hair curling around her face. "Right on time," Trish chirps, reaching for my carry-on and slinging it over her shoulder with the ease of someone who works out regularly. Where are her glasses? Now I remember: She decided contacts are more youthful. "It's dog eat dog," she'd told me during one of our infrequent phone conversations, her voice low and agitated. "Ageism is alive and kicking. You've no idea how hard an older woman has to work to keep her job, much less get ahead." Trish speaks in trendy phrases, a habit she acquired while temping for a PR firm. She never lets me forget I'm out of the loop, a homemaker living off my retired husband's generous pension. In her eyes, I'm lazy and privileged. In my eyes, she's a dippy lady who can never decide what she wants to do, or who she wants to do it to. Last year she told fortunes, her identity shielded by a 900 number. Now, it seems, she's a caseworker. "I've had it with the psychic hotline," she explains. "I'm into deadbeat dads." I have an image of my sister in a London Fog, packing a piece.

"Are we going straight to Mom's?" I ask. This will be my first chance to see the retirement complex that Trish describes as a residence hotel for single women.

She stuffs my bag in her hatchback and ushers me into the passenger seat. "She's planned lunch. We wouldn't want to mess with cream of tomato and melted cheese now, would we?" This comfort fare from our childhood, Mom's idea of a treat, brings back memories. Does Trish still leave the crusts? I can't wait to see.

Last time Mom and I were together we fought over Aunt Jessie's porcelain bowl, which Mom intended for Trish to inherit. As a child, I always liked to run my fingers around the inside of that bowl, tracing the tiny swirls that lay beneath the brilliant cobalt glaze. Pop used to display it proudly, claiming it was a collector's item, worth "a penny or two." Through the years, it was the one keepsake I coveted; Trish had never liked it, so why would she care? "But Jessie would have wanted Trish to have it," Mom insisted. "Why dispute the dead?"

I argued that Pop's sister Jessie hardly knew us. The one time she came east to visit, Trish and I had chicken pox and were in quarantine. We made sheet tents and camped on the porch. The dogwoods were in bloom. The bluebirds were nesting. By the time I raised this memory from our dusty past, Mom and I were burnt out from the effort of grieving for my father. We'd spent days sorting through possessions accumulated over fifty-five years of marriage. Her house was on the market. She had convinced herself she was ready to abdicate, but she was in no mood to compromise. I wrapped the bowl with as much care as I could muster and shipped the package, uninsured, to my sister.

Mom's residence hotel is a tidy, no-frills affair, a sturdy assemblage with brick-fronted units and curved benches that frame the entrance like parentheses. "When it's sunny," Trish comments, "you can't buy a seat out here." I imagine little old ladies scrunched together like sparrows on a wire, feathered hats ruffling in the breeze. "Hello, Hazel," Trish says cheerfully, greeting a tiny, wizened woman flanked by two others inside the entranceway. Hopeful looks illuminate their finely chiseled, pruny faces. *Will someone please come and rescue us?* is the message they seem to be sending. "A little slow," Trish whispers, "but sweet." A front-desk aide sits reading a romance novel sandwiched between cover illustrations of Fabio flexing his pecs, a swoony nude drooping at his side. "Hello, Marge. I like that sweater! That's *definitely* your color." My sister the personality girl is working the crowd, something she's done her whole life. Can't they see she doesn't give a shit? But no, they sparkle like crystal, refracting her charm.

We puzzle our way through a dark maze of carpeted corridors labeled with the names of trees: Oak Lane, Maple Grove, Birch Drive. Mom's is Pine Way. We stop in front of a door ornamented by a beribboned whisk broom bearing her name in neat calligraphy, an art Trish perfected in her post-hippie phase. Other doors are equally festooned: a twig wreath dotted with dried flowers, a stuffed gingham cat, a perky straw boater with grosgrain dripping from its brim. It's clear that in Columbus, daughters knock themselves out, *Good Housekeeping*–wise.

After Trish turns her key in the lock, we step into a kitchenette, where the appliances are scaled down for limited production. Cooking for me, myself, and I, as Trish might say. No banquets are prepared here; the ladies take their evening meal in a central dining area. "Mom?" Trish calls. "We're here." Through a doorway I can see her, napping. We step into the bedroom, where the fluffy decor reflects my sister's tastes—pink flounces everywhere, a little girl's fantasy isle of scalloped hems. "Her hearing aid's turned off," Trish notes, reaching down to tap Mom's arm. "Hey. Sleepyhead. Look who's here." She mouths the words generously, obviously used to translating silences.

Mom opens her eyes. "Oh," she says, seeing Trish and smiling. "It's *you*. Where's . . ."

For a minute my heart freezes: She doesn't remember me. Then

I remember Pop's pauses. "Sometimes it takes awhile for things to float up," he used to apologize, melting into sweetness in his old age, too late for amends, "sometimes I need a little help." I move into her field of vision. She's still fuzzy from sleep. "Hey, Mom. It's Mary." When I bend to kiss her, she smells of vanilla, her skin's natural scent (I swear), bringing with it my childhood. I want to feel warm again, encompassed in the fleece of her love. Won't she smile at me? While I wait for her face to soften I say, "*You* look good. I can see that apartment life is agreeing with you," figuring a compliment should earn me some points.

She sits up slowly. "Whoo, dizzy. Don't know why. Taking that new blood-pressure medicine, I guess. Did Trish tell you I'm now on blood-pressure medicine, for high when I've always had low? Is that crazy? I have this new doctor, young mother, don't know how her kids will grow up, in daycare I suppose, thinks she knows everything about aging. Wants me to call her by her first name."

Trish winks at me. "The doctor's terrific, actually," she whispers. "Gerontology is the Specialty of the Future, you know. Don't let Mom fool you into thinking she doesn't like Dr. Muriel."

Mom is standing up now, leaning on her walker, clumping her way out of the gloomy bedroom, where slanted blinds keep out the dim light of a winter's day. In the living room I detect further traces of Trish. Her paintings, a by-product of therapy, circle the room: the gaudy, grinning clown; the apple trees in over-bloom; the peaches feverish and plump, spilling out of their basket. In life as in her art, Trish rarely stints. Tears come to my eyes as I remember my sister proudly displaying her still life at the hospital art show, where the peaches took first prize.

I can't help wishing there was something of me in this room. But, no reason to get all worked up, I tell myself. I'm out of favor now, but Mom will get over it, and when she does, photos of my children will once again adorn her end tables. Wait. Is that the little Royal Doulton rose I gave her? I figured it had vanished with the rest of her knickknacks sold to bargain-browsers at church bazaars.

"There's no point in saving these," she'd said one day after we fought, indicating every single piece of jewelry, every curio I'd ever wrapped for her birthday. The sight of the rescued china rose makes me feel better. At least there's something connecting me to this dollhouse my sister has furnished.

"You'll sleep here," Mom says, pointing to the couch. "A pull-out. I hope you'll be comfortable. The bedding's in there." She indicates a closet, really a pantry, whose interior reveals an assortment of favorite grocery items I can see with my eyes closed: Cream of Wheat, dried apricots, Betty Crocker instant potatoes, canned lima beans, and Mom's one luxury (inherited from Pop), imported thick-cut marmalade. "It has to be the one with the ship on the label," my father used to say, handing me their shopping list. By then he'd stopped driving and was spending most days in bed. Reluctantly he, who since his retirement had done everything, even the shopping, was relying on me to run their household. "Mary, my angel," he'd flirt, "you're the one I can count on." *Right.* By then, Trish was a thousand miles away, out of his way for good. "Family therapy? A shrink telling me what to do? When hell freezes." Stubborn, nasty old Irish coot. In the last year, he was a pain. Very particular. Always having to have a certain brand of this or that, like marmalade. "If you can't get the one with the ship, forget it." I'd search the shelves until I found a ceramic crock of marmalade with a clipper ship on the label. The one and only.

"Fine. I'm sure I'll be very comfortable," I reply. I'm talking to a stranger here, a bellhop showing me to my hotel room. How much shall I tip? "Is there any special place you'd like me to put my suitcase, Mom?"

Mom and Trish have their heads together. "Tomorrow night, then," Trish says. "I'll keep it simple. And I'll talk to her about the car. I can't promise." I figure I might as well be someplace else, the way they're talking, then Trish remembers I'm there. "You'll come for dinner at my place tomorrow night? Good. And, uh, *we* think it'd be real helpful if you'd rent a car," she suggests gaily. "We'll have to go back out to the airport, but as you've seen, it isn't far. I have to scoot to the office, but I can come back later, pick you up. Then you can follow me to my place, see where it is in daylight. You never could follow directions! Don't worry, it's not far, I'll even draw you a map. I'd ask you in for a drink, but I've got something going for tonight . . ."

Doesn't she even blush when she brags about sex? What happened to the last lover? What's it like, I wonder, to be Trish, with her long string of enviable Somethings? I think of my own long, up-and-down journey with the same guy. Thirty years. That's something going.

"Hey. I haven't even asked you," she says as she backs out the door. "How's Fred, anyway? And the kids. I can't believe they're in college! Where did the years go?"

At the Avis counter, Trish can't contain herself. "No, not there, sign *there,*" she says, and pushes my hand to the left corner of the contract. "I can't believe you've never done this before. That Fred! He probably does everything for you."

"Oh, yeah, sure," I say, feeling testy. "Everything." My little sister. After all these years of me telling her what to do, she's getting even. Now, with Mom practically living on her doorstep, she thinks she has the upper hand. The young salesclerk hides behind too much makeup and a weary, pasted-on smile. She asks me if I'll need a map. "I have a personal guide," I say sharply, nodding at Trish. "This is *her* town. She's the one who knows all the one-way streets in Columbus."

"Don't forget to fill 'er up before you return," says the girl warily. Trish behaves as though I'm a preteen, so it's no wonder the salesgirl's eyes mirror her distrust.

That evening, Mom decides we'll eat in. The Barbie-kitchen meal is a simple affair, straight from the freezer, a choice of chicken with angel-hair pasta or oriental beef with noodles. "You pick the one you want," she says, greedily eyeing the beef. I pick the beef.

She nukes our dinners in the little microwave and sets the table with cheap china flocked with floral nosegays, again nothing I recognize, obviously Trish's idea of what someone should buy when starting life over for the very last time. The handles of the utensils are bright green Melamine to match the leaves of the potted ivy.

In the living room, we sit on the flocked floral couch, separated by canyons of spite. I wonder whose pain is deeper, and who will bridge the gap first? We sip our drinks from green glass goblets. "Try saying *that* three times in a row," I joke lamely. For the special occasion, Mom asked Trish to purchase a bottle of single-malt Scotch. My sister's clown painting stares down at me. I stare back, not wanting to turn and find myself reflected in Mom's sad, thick-lens-distorted eyes. I notice she can no longer see well enough to know if she's spilled something on her clothing. In her closet, I see evidence of prior meals splattered on knit tops and blouses. I'll say something to Trish, suggest she eyeball Mom's wardrobe once a week, send things to the cleaners, buy a bottle of Woolite to keep near the bathroom sink. When Mom lived near me, I'd check on these details. "You got a drying rack?" I ask. Maybe I'll launder some sweaters before I go home. Show up Trish.

I devour fake Chinese. In the time it takes Mom to push bogus Italian from one side of the plate to the other, she tells me about Aunt Helen, who has recently lost a son to cancer. I remember Cousin Donald as a wimpy little kid who whined a lot. There's no end to the gloom that emanates from Mom's family: Aunt Liz has Alzheimer's; Uncle Jack is confined to bed because of an old back injury. When she's finished reciting the litany of sorrows, half her dinner remains on the plate. "Would you like some dessert?" she asks. "I have no-fat sherbet and low-fat wafers." She should be eating a regular diet, I think. She's lost so much weight since Pop died. I can tell from her face, which was never so angular, and her clothes, which drip from her skinny shoulders like ill-hung drapes. Doesn't Trish see any of this? Can't she take Mom shopping for new clothes that fit?

As if she's reading my mind, Mom says, "There's a big mall two blocks away. While you're here, since you have a car, if it isn't too much trouble, I'd like a few things."

"Sure. Is there anything else you'd like to do? Downtown, maybe?"

"What would I do downtown?"

"I don't know. Whatever you do with Trish. A museum. Lunch."

"She's too busy for museums. And besides, I can't see the paintings anymore, so why bother? And as for lunch, the mall has plenty of places." She pushes away her bowl of half-eaten sherbet. A rosy glacier in thaw, the raspberry pool widens to float a wafer-raft. Mom sighs. "It's not like in the old days, when your father and I used to take trips." She picks up her spoon and drags it through the melted sherbet, making a path to nowhere.

That night there's a frost, and the next morning I use a green-handled knife to scrape the windshield of my rented Nissan while Mom waits, bundled in her too-big coat, inside the front door of the complex. The prunies chatter like birds on a wire, but with her hat pulled down over her hearing aid, she can't hear them. Instead, she admires her boots, a Christmas gift from Trish. *I* sent her the boots, I tell her. Doesn't she remember? They came from Filene's, her favorite store. Oh, she says. I don't remember anything these days. My gloves are wet through, my hands cold as I guide her over the slippery spots to the car. Does Trish ever take her on winter errands? I ask.

We arrive at the mall as it's opening, and I settle her into a wheelchair provided for handicapped shoppers. "This won't do," she says. "There's no footrest. Oh, never mind. I'll just hold them up." She sticks out her legs as if to admire the famous boots. "We'll just have to be careful around corners." In a Gap, I'm reminded that the hearing-impaired don't know how loudly they're speaking. As we make our way through stacks of sweaters, Mom's voice startles the preppy salesclerk. "Who would buy this stuff?" she asks, plucking a sweatshirt from its cubicle. "Would you?"

"Where to?" I shout, back on the mall's main drag. We pass a bed-and-bath emporium where mermaids swim from wires and fish sport Disney smiles. Trish has furnished Mom with towels whose eyelet-ruffled borders scratch the skin. Typically, she chooses things that look good but aren't very practical.

"No place special. Just to look."

"I thought you said . . ."

"Oh, I don't want to bother with that now. I can do that anytime. Jennifer, the girl who comes to help me, can bring me over. I don't want to waste your time." She brakes with her feet, and the chair comes to a shuddering halt. "Let's do something *you* want to do."

Three hours later, we've startled the salesladies in almost every store in the mall, left our half-eaten lunch on a tiny table in the fast-food court, and checked out the lingerie and hosiery boutiques twice. My head is pounding, and Mom is getting on my nerves. "Don't they make panty girdles anymore? Where are the aprons?" She is forever searching for out-of-stock items, a habit; she wouldn't be my mother if she ever found what she was looking for, or if she ever looked for something that could be found. "They don't have the socks with the high, ribbed cuffs anymore," she whines. "I can't wear the others. Look at these cups," she says after trying on ten different styles of bras. "What am I, a freak that I can't find any cups to fit my bosoms?" The salesclerk waits discreetly outside the swinging doors of the changing room. In a space barely big enough to accommodate the wheelchair and me, we've managed to make quite a mess. We're surrounded by our bunched-up overcoats and our solitary purchase, a small leather change purse wrapped in layers of tissue paper, nestled in the oversized shopping bag Mom insists on carrying ("in case we buy anything else"). Bras hang from every available hook, like aviator's goggles. My mother, Amelia Earhart in her wheelchair cockpit, seems prepared to vanish in this sea of tricot. "Let's get out of here," she shouts. From beyond the shuttered doors comes an audible sigh of relief.

I've seen Trish's house only once, when Fred and I were on our way back from vacationing in California. At that point Trish was married to Joe, an airline pilot several years younger than she (never specific, she said "several," though from the way she described him, I would have guessed more). Joe was flying that week, and there'd been an unscheduled layover on the coast because of bad weather, so we spent the evening alone with Trish. "We've just finished redecorating. What do you think?" she asked the minute we were inside the door. "We're crazy about the Southwest. I chose all your basic earth tones. To give that feeling of warmth and comfort, yet spaciousness. And the Indian art." In a large framed print above the couch, women displayed their beads at an open market. "Don't you just love R. C. Gorman? It's a copy, of course," Trish confided. Opposite, spotlights showcased a wall hanging. "Navajo. Pricey, but these things are worth it." A dining room mural featured twin saguaros poking their spines into a desert sunset. "Joe insisted. You don't think it's tacky, do you?" I shook my head. "Good, because I really tried to capture the authentic feel. Of course I had help, a fabulous firm in Phoenix," Trish confessed. "They'll get you absolutely anything you want. For a price, of course."

"Of course," I echoed, wondering how they'd managed to pay for it all. I knew Joe made a good salary as a pilot, but I also knew Trish wasn't working.

That night my sister taught Fred to tango. "C'mere, Fred. Let me teach you how. Ta da dum dum dum. That's it!" As they twirled and dipped their way around the room, narrowly missing the clay pots ("Pueblo, very fragile, *mucho dinero*"), I sulked on the sofa, recalling the times I'd tried to get Fred to take me dancing. "Oh, don't be such a poop," Trish said, pulling me to my feet. "You guys should take a cruise. They have lessons in things you don't even *want* to learn!" She placed my hand in Fred's. "Put your left hand on his shoulder. That's the ticket, sis!" I was back in fifth-grade gym class, where we had to dance with boys once a month.

I could feel Fred's muscles twitch beneath my fingers. In the background, fiery music heated up the room: ta da dum dum *dum*! "Fred, you're a natural. Mare, loosen up. There. Isn't that fun?" Nose to nose, cheek to cheek, we moved to the rhythms of the dance of love. Fred was breathing hard. Before long, I'd bruised my shin on a collector's item. "I bet you've never had so much fun!" Trish said, cutting in.

Fred was grinning like a Cheshire cat. That night, I watched my sister go fishing for my husband. She reeled him in, gave him the once-over, then tossed him, gasping for air, back into my pond. She'd perfected the sport. With a new lure—a brand-new, lighter shade of blond and a halo of soft, springy curls—she affected the look of a Botticelli angel. Grudgingly, I could imagine her marrying a man ten years her junior, and him not caring that she had crow's feet or cellulite.

A couple of months later, Trish discovered Joe had been refueling with a seventeen-year-old fashion model. "That son of a bitch," she hissed over the phone. "Can you believe I fell for his shit?"

She was crying. I felt sorry for her. I knew she'd only been teasing that night she made a play for Fred. I wanted to say something to make her feel better, to make her pain go away. When we were little and Pop blew his stack, I'd try to console her. She'd come into my bed and we'd cuddle. "What did you do to make him so mad?" I'd ask, but she'd only shrug her shoulders.

"Some people seem to collect trouble," was Mom's cool response when I told her about Joe, but I saw in her eyes the sad, empty stare I remembered from childhood, acknowledging Trish's pain, yet denying responsibility for it. *What can* I *do?* she seemed to be saying.

Now, as Mom and I step through Trish's front door, I notice a whole new look, very West Coast. If I were my sister's publicist, her brochure might read: *Splashes of bright color invade the senses. The Spanish tiles are strewn with persimmon-hued cushions, invoking a casual atmosphere. On the draperies and slipcovers, lush hibiscus blooms proliferate.* This look, like the one before it, hasn't come cheap. "Wow," I say. "You've put a whole lot into this, girl."

"Yeah, well. I needed a change."

"I guess there's a fortune in tracking delinquent dads."

"Very funny." Trish is stuffing cherry tomatoes, jamming crab salad into each tiny cavity. "Don't worry, I'm not using the money you send to Mom. I cashed in some stocks. Stuff Pop had put aside. Ask her if you don't believe me."

On the plane I swore I wouldn't lose my temper, but now anger flashes through me, a Pac-man gobbling my resolve. Just last month Mom told me she couldn't meet her expenses. It hadn't occurred to me that Mom's best girl might be dipping into the till. I watch Trish stuff those little tomatoes with such force their skins split. *Look what you've made me do.*

"You should feel sorry for your sister," Mom has told me. "You have a husband and children. What has *she* got?"

I remember an SOS call from the Kingdom of Light, a few days before Trish's nineteenth birthday. "I'm pregnant," she sobbed. I borrowed a friend's car and drove up north where I found her huddled outside a sagging tepee, waiting to be rescued. For the first time in my life, I wasn't envious. Her pressing needs—a bath, wholesome meals, and a new set of values—declared to me that beauty was a burden. I saw her through the abortion, which wiped out my meager savings. "Don't tell Pop," she begged. And Mom? Like a good sister, I never said a word to either of them.

I carry a plate of battered tomatoes into the living room, where Mom waits like a duchess for her hors d'oeuvres. "Hasn't your sister done a wonderful job with this place?" she asks, but I'm already back in the kitchen, ready to assist the chef.

Trish lines up glasses on a tray, fills them evenly with bottled water, and allows me to distribute ice cubes. "Not too many," she cautions, in control again. "We don't want to have a spill now, do we? Remember Pop? He had a thing about spills. So put only two cubes in each glass."

"Speaking of spills," I say. Mom is wearing a sweater that recalls past mishaps. "I notice she's not seeing well enough to keep clean. D'you think you could maybe keep closer tabs on that?"

Trish curls her long, pale pink fingernails inward in an *I-won't* gesture I recognize from our childhood: tiny fists curled in defiance of me—*I won't pick up the toys, I won't go first at the dentist, I won't let you play with my doll.* "Like what? You think I don't have enough to do already? *You* try running her life and staying on top of a sixty-hour-a-week job." When she slaps the counter for emphasis, the water jiggles, spilling up over the tops of two glasses. It seems two cubes is too many, after all.

"Well, it wasn't my idea to have her move out here. You two cooked up that scheme. I thought Mom should stay in the East, where she's always lived. Where she's at least near people who mattered to her and Pop."

"What're you two chattering about?" Mom yells.

"She's not *that* deaf," I notice, but Trish is shoving a tray of Pepperidge Farm finger rolls in the oven, stubbornly refusing to use a mitt, trying to prove she's invincible.

The next day, my last of the visit, crawls by at a turtle's pace. To ease the strain I try to think of ways to help, little chores that might assist my mother in her new digs. "How about I line your shelves?" I suggest. "I see you never had a chance to do that. I can run out and buy some paper and it'll be done in a jiff."

"Why bother? I'll just have to remove it when they paint. They paint every other year. They're very good about upkeep here. It's a nice place." She pauses, then adds, "Very clean."

"Very clean," I echo, the hurt of being so unilaterally shut out of her life preventing me from injecting enthusiasm. I want to tell her I miss her but the words won't come. My way of paying her back for leaving Rhode Island. Thing is, I *do* miss her. I miss her needing me. Call it empty nest. Fred says I don't know when I'm well off.

While she watches her soap opera, I pick her address book off the kitchen table to thumb through the well-worn pages. The names and addresses of friends and relatives, now deceased, evoke memories. Others have relocated, but their new addresses, recorded in Pop's palsied, illegible scrawl, may as well be Heaven or Hell. Maybe I can clean up this mess, I think. Neaten things up. So I tug the blank pages from the back and start copying, eliminating the friends and acquaintances who no longer exist on this planet. Under R are all the restaurants she and Pop ever patronized; under D, all the doctors and dentists they ever consulted. Why save any of these names? I copy and crumple, copy and crumple. She'll be pleased, I know. I'm doing her a favor, something that will remind her of me after I've gone home.

The program over, she comes into the kitchen, bumps her walker into the dropleaf, and stands over me. "What are you doing?" she asks.

"I'm redoing your address book. It was a mess."

"Oh." She grips the top of the walker so tightly that her knuckles whiten. In this gesture I see where my sister started curling her nails until they cut her palms. Oh, yes. I remember now: Mom doesn't like it when I manage her life. I look through the magnifying lenses into the large pupils of her eyes and there I read her silent rejoinder: *But it was* my *mess.*

The phone rings early next morning, jolting me to a sitting position within reach of the Princess phone my parents used to keep on their bedside table, a familiar memento I'd failed to notice. As I pull the phone onto my lap I notice their old number, in my handwriting, on the base.

"Good. You're up," Trish says. "Are you sure you can find your way back to Avis? I could lead you." *You never were any good at directions.*

"I'll be fine," I insist. "Really. I have your map, remember?"

She laughs. "Oh, yeah. You'll never get lost with that scribbly thing."

I feel I have to say it. "Thanks for everything."

"But I . . ."

"You know what I mean."

"You'd do the same."

And did, for so many years. And never took a penny. "She can be a handful."

"You never did figure her out."

"I suppose you've got all the answers."

"Not all, but some."

"She owes you. Is that it? For all those times Pop went after you and she stood by, never lifting a finger to stop him?"

"She couldn't. I accept that."

"Well, you're more forgiving than I'd be."

For a moment I hear only the sucking of air, the sound Trish makes when she inhales. Then she says, "I owe you a lot, you know."

"Meaning?"

"The day I dropped Aunt Jessie's bowl. We were racing around, playing one of those crazy chasing games, remember? I knocked it off the sideboard. I didn't break it, just chipped the bottom. Unless you knew where to look, you'd never notice."

"Oh, Trish, I do remember! You were screaming, so afraid of what would happen when Pop found out. You were right to be scared. He came after you with his belt, the one with the killer buckle."

"You tried to stop him."

Don't, Daddy. You'll hurt her. That time he left the scar, a keepsake she'd have for the rest of her life. "God! You must have thought I was crazy for sending you that bowl. It was Mom who insisted. She said Jessie would have wanted you to have it," I explain. "You know how Mom is always trying to make up for Pop's treatment of you, as if a bowl could blot out the bruises."

"To hear Mom talk, Pop never had a temper."

"Christ. He had the shortest fuse! But why always you? Why never me?"

"You were smarter," Trish says with conviction. "Better behaved."

"I never got caught." I shudder, remembering other times: doors slamming, Trish screaming, me knowing what was going on but feeling helpless to prevent it. *Some people just attract trouble.* "I have to ask you. The bowl. Did you smash it? I wouldn't blame you."

She laughs. "Would you believe some sucker paid forty bucks for it at my yard sale? Forty bucks! Hey. Don't tell me *you* wanted it."

"No way," I lie, thinking it was funny the way Pop had a thing about that ugly bowl, treating it like a family heirloom when it was obviously a piece of junk. *Jessie was very special to your dad. When your grandparents died, he raised her.* "Do you think Pop was as hard on Jessie as he was on you?"

"Who cares? Hey, sis. I didn't mean for things to get so heavy on your last morning here." I can hear the flick of a lighter, the suck of air, the pause, then the exhale. She told me she had quit smoking. At her place, she'd hidden the ashtrays. Poor Trish. Always getting caught. "Take care, Mary."

"*You* take care."

"Have to. No Fred!" she chuckles. "Tell the kids to write their auntie Trish. Ah! Who am I kidding? Kids don't write." She takes a deep drag, then lets it out slowly. "Do they?"

"Come see us. We have a cottage for the month of July. You and I can cruise the beach and pick up punks."

She laughs. "Maybe. We'll see. Love you." Flippant, yet from the heart. Trish's style.

When we were kids we made a pact—*together always in all ways*—but Mom, wanting to compensate for Pop's harsh treatment of Trish, drove a wedge between us. "Love you." I toss the words back at my sister, meaning them, wanting to add, "*only* you," loud enough for Mom to hear.

Before I put the phone back on the bookcase, I run my finger gently over the number I used to call at least four times a day while Mom was still my responsibility, my big baby.

"Was that Trish?" Mom asks, hobbling to the doorway of her room. "I wish I'd known. There was something I wanted to ask her."

In her hands are my towels from the bathroom, ready to be laundered. The sheets will follow, whipped from the mattress and rolled tight to fit inside the pillowcase. Soon there'll be nothing left to mark my visit. A child once more, my hurt feels as palpable as the scar on Trish's thigh. Ask *me,* I want to say. Ask *me.*

THE ELF GIG

Sometimes I think it's unfair that my father died of a stroke in his fifties, leaving a midget and a woman with rheumatoid arthritis to fend for themselves. At the funeral my mother and sister cried like babies while I, conscious of everyone's stares, tried to be dignified. Familiar phrases like "child-size, but her sister's perfectly normal," though they used to cause pain, now seemed to describe someone else. Curious onlookers, seeing me for the first time, turned away and pretended to look at my father in his coffin. People should know better than to stare at me, because I'm obviously not a freak, just a very small person. I want to say to them, "Do you think it's fun to have to buy your clothes in Children's Chubettes or to have to sit on a telephone book when you go to a restaurant?"

At the radio station where I work as an advertising copywriter, I'm valued for my ability to write. No one has ever made an issue of my size. So when the station manager asked me to be Santa's elf at the Salvation Army, where we're doing a remote broadcast the day before Christmas, I said yes. Ralph Mooney, the manager, made it seem like an honor to be selected to hand out presents to the needy. He said his wife had volunteered to make me a costume. He also said he wanted my role as an elf to be a surprise, and he asked me not to tell anyone.

It wasn't until I talked it over with Carrie, the news director, that I had second thoughts. Carrie had to know the details because it was her job to coordinate talent for that particular broadcast. She's a sensitive soul, concerned about violating the rights of practically everyone, from acrobats to zebras. "What are you, exhibit A?" she asked. "Mooney's exploiting you. You *have* to say no."

"I can't. The missus is making me a costume. Besides, who will do it if I don't?" I'm thinking, if Carrie's right, I'll be the Town Clown.

"You're hopeless," Carrie said with a sigh. "What am I going to do with you?"

Christmas is approaching. Business is picking up. Everything has to have a holiday theme, which poses a problem for me. How many different ways can you say "Merry Christmas"? At the moment, I'm composing ten-second greetings to present to clients, simple little phrases, easy to write. There isn't much you can say in twenty-five words and still include the client's name and address. The challenge is to make the greetings catchy and, at the same time, impart a feeling of goodwill. For instance, it isn't enough to simply say, "A Merry Christmas and a Happy New Year from your friends at Charles Toyota, 15 Green Street, Anytown." A better choice would be: "Merry Christmas from Al and his service team at Charles Toyota."

Christmas is the most lucrative time of year in advertising. The only other time that seems to rival it is when there's an election. Then all the candidates run ads that say something like, "Paid for by the friends of Calvin Crowell. Marvin Flack, fiscal agent."

One aspect of this job that really appeals to me is the friendly office atmosphere. It's as though we've all been working together for years. On someone's birthday, we order a cake and take the time to celebrate. When one of the deejays turned twenty-three, we interrupted his show and sang to him. The listeners loved it. When the receptionist was ill, we took up a collection and sent her flowers. The management is very appreciative, too; I've been told we'll get a

Christmas bonus. I can certainly use mine. I want to give my sister a food processor, and they're expensive.

The other day, Carrie asked me to have lunch with her. She has a graduate degree in communications from a big eastern university, so I didn't really know what we'd talk about, but as it turns out, we do share common interests. For instance, we both enjoy reading historical fiction. My favorite period is Elizabethan England, with all its florid intrigues, while Carrie prefers novels set in an earlier time. We spent most of our lunch hour comparing writers—Jean Plaidy vs. Thomas Costain, for instance, and I told her I never tire of reading about Mary, Queen of Scots. I get sad whenever I think of the scenario that preceded her execution. She met her fate with great dignity and a certain grace. Everyone present later testified to her courage. The hardest part for me was the little Skye terrier that stayed beneath her skirts until the beheading, then later starved itself to death because of a broken heart. Carrie said there's a limit to pathos, that at any given point it can be said to exceed the bounds of literary decency. I like to wring every drop of emotion from a good dramatic scene, but then, I've always been a dreamer.

I admire Carrie because she's intelligent and just aggressive enough to get ahead without turning people off. She dresses in a very professional manner, and always looks nicely groomed. Yesterday, we drew names for the Christmas party, and I got hers. I'm going to give her a bottle of Blue Nun. We can choose to give either joke gifts or the real thing, and I'd rather give her something she can enjoy. Those of us who are single have been told we can bring a guest. Carrie said I should bring my mother, but I certainly wouldn't do that, because my mother moves like a turtle and complains constantly about the soreness in her joints. She hates going out at night because the cold air aggravates her condition. She has to make a fist to hold her utensils when she eats, and, because she's put on so much weight, it takes two people to lift her out of a chair. We make quite a pair. To tell the truth, I think we embarrass each other.

Carrie said she and her date would pick me up and take me home, and I thanked her. If she hadn't offered me a ride, I don't think I could go. I certainly can't ask Mr. Strauss, who gives me a lift to and from work (he says it's no extra trouble, since he lives in our building and my office is on his way). I give him gas money, but getting a lift to work is one thing and getting a ride to a party is another. Besides, Mrs. Strauss, who looks like a large dumpling with legs, seems very protective of her mister and might object.

I have an occasional fantasy in which I fall in love with a younger, thinner Mr. Strauss. We drive up to Canada and make love in a Niagara Falls motel. I chose Niagara Falls because I've been there—not with a lover, but with my mother, many years ago when I was about fourteen. I remember everything about that trip—the way the water sounds like thunder, and how hard it is to move freely through the crowds of people. I remember being afraid to look down into the great space that separated me from the water. My mother tried to lift me up so I could see over the railing, but I resisted. I started to cry. She said I was ruining her day. Aside from that moment, I have good memories of Niagara Falls. In my fantasy, Strauss is a good lover, masterful (as the novels say), which means, I suppose, that he knows all the right techniques. In the books I read, women frequently close their eyes during lovemaking, but in my fantasy I don't close mine, because I don't want to miss anything that's going on.

Here, distractions abound. The station is noisy, and my workstation is right in the middle of all the action. If I'm not careful, I could get behind, and then, elf or no, I'd lose my job.

The salespeople will be back shortly, bringing more orders. I can feel the muscles in my shoulders starting to bunch. By the time I get home tonight, I'll be too tired to cope with Ma and all her complaining. She'll have the jars all lined up for me to open. It isn't that she doesn't try to hold up her end of the housekeeping (she'll start dinner, for instance), but I always get an earful the minute I step inside the door: Someone tried to deliver a package but she couldn't slide back the locking bolt; the phone rang twelve times but she still didn't get there in time, et cetera.

I've already decided I won't tell her about Mooney's scheme. She'd be much worse than Carrie. She'd never let me forget that I'd been exploited. Of course, I can remember that she kept pushing me around in a stroller for years after I was able to walk. She kept me a baby for as long as she dared, even when my younger sister Alice was around to be coddled. Although my real name is Christina, she calls me Teeny, not Tina like everybody else.

On second thought, I'll have to tell her.

Karen, the receptionist, has been using the phone all afternoon. I can tell they're personal calls, because she keeps her voice down low. I can't hear what she's saying, but she gets this silly, soft look when she talks to her honey, Bart. Karen says Bart's wife is an alcoholic who refuses to give him a divorce. Karen told me he calls her on his lunch hour from a pay phone. Once when he called, Karen was away from her desk, so I answered. "Is Karen there?" he asked in a nice, deep voice.

"No," I replied. "She just stepped out for a minute."

"Bummer," he said, and hung up. It was the first time I'd heard an adult use that expression.

When Karen returned, I told her about the call she missed. She said Bart was planning to take her south sometime during the winter, but she didn't say when or how. It sounds pretty romantic, but I'd hate to be Karen when his wife finds out.

From my window I can see glowing streetlights. People are bending into the late-afternoon wind, jamming their hands in their pockets, holding their briefcases tightly against their sides. It will be cold waiting on the corner for Strauss.

If Mooney would just return from his meeting, I could tell him I've changed my mind about the elf gig. I can usually tell when he's coming up the stairs by the way Karen snaps to attention. She sits bolt upright and squeaks her chair, and by the time he stands in front of her desk, she's the picture of industry, clicking away at the keyboard, logging the next day's programs.

Squeak goes the chair, and I hop off my stool. "Mr. Mooney, may I have a word with you?" I say as he moves into the corridor, red-faced, breathing hard. He's carrying a package that he waves in my face.

"Got something to show you," he says. "Wait till you see. You're gonna love it. You gotta try it on right away so I can tell the missus if it has to be altered." He unwraps the package and I see red and green material, my elf costume. I'm thinking the missus must have stayed up all night to finish it. "There!" he says triumphantly, shaking the jumpsuit so that its legs dance a furious little jig. "Isn't that just the cat's meow?"

Karen pops up from her chair and runs over to Mooney. She takes one arm of the suit and they play tug-of-war while I stand by, feeling neglected. It *is* my suit, after all. "Careful! You'll stretch it out of shape," I admonish them. The next thing I know, I'm grabbing it away. It feels soft and springy, like a baby's stretch sleeper. My niece has one just like it, only not in red and green, of course.

"Did you ever in all your life see anything so cute?" Karen gushes. "Put it on, put it on!" She jumps up and down like a cheerleader.

"You can use my office," Mooney says hopefully.

Carrie, where are you when I need you? Ah, yes. She's on air, delivering the five o'clock news.

Karen bounces up and down like a kangaroo. "Put it on! Put in on!" she squeals.

There's no way I'm going to put it on here. "Um, why don't I just take it home? That way, if there's anything that needs adjusting, my mother can fix it."

Mooney's shoulders slump. "No, no. That won't do. The missus said . . ."

"Come *on*," Karen stage-whispers. "Don't disappoint him."

Mooney clasps his hands together, pleading.

I simply can't do this. "My ride comes in a couple of minutes. If I'm not on time, he'll leave without me," I explain, hoping he'll understand.

Resignation clouds Mooney's face as he hands me the plastic wrapper. "You'll want this to keep it clean. The missus says to put it on carefully, like panty hose, to avoid runs."

Karen giggles.

As I fold the costume I notice the toes have red pom-poms on them, a nice touch. It's obvious the missus has put a lot of effort into making it. Mooney has put one arm into his overcoat and is groping for the second sleeve. Karen is talking in low tones again, the telephone receiver wedged between her shoulder and her cheek. Through the loudspeaker I can hear Perry Como singing "The Lord's Prayer," signaling sign-off. I can also hear the deejays arguing loudly; Mel Smith is complaining because Harvey Clark, the program director, has scheduled him to work on New Year's Day. Mooney utters a sigh of frustration and uses his key to open the outside door, which is kept double-locked after five. Cold air salted with snowflakes rushes in. When we part, we each wave goodbye.

Strauss is waiting at the corner, his car wreathed by plumes of thick white exhaust. As I hurry to meet him, I'm careful not to slip on the sidewalk, where a film of new-fallen snow coats the pavement. I open the door and climb into the front seat.

He shakes his head. "Five minutes late tonight. Do you know that?" I expect a scolding, but none comes. Instead, he pulls away from the curb and heads toward Main Street, where yesterday's heavy snow crowns the Christmas decorations that hang from the street lamps, adding a scenic touch. "Whatcha got?" he asks, noticing the parcel. "Early present from the boyfriend?"

"You could call it that," I answer coyly. This is part of the game we play. He likes to imagine me in bed with the voices he hears on the station, and I like to imagine him in bed with me. "Mind if I turn on the radio?" In deference to me, he keeps the dial set at the station. We listen to the Christophers' message for the day, followed by an invitation to tune in tomorrow, followed by static and the faint wail of rock music issuing from a city station that bleeds through on this frequency after hours.

I begin to worry about what my mother will say when she sees the costume. She'll probably laugh. I won't get upset. I'll try to think of how Mary, Queen of Scots, would handle the situation. There is, I've discovered from my reading, a way to turn the worst situations into triumphs. I was planning to wait until late evening to model the suit, but now I think I'll change as soon as I get home, and start things off on a lively note.

"Penny for your thoughts?" Strauss asks, slowing down as the traffic light turns yellow. In his overcoat and woolen cap he looks a little like my father. Snowflakes fly against the windshield. Strauss, a careful driver, increases the speed of the wipers and clears the condensation from inside the window by passing his gloved hand back and forth against the glass.

"Not for sale." I reach inside the wrapping to caress the soft material. In the silence that follows, I try to picture the children who'll be waiting for me at the Salvation Army. No doubt they'll love meeting an elf. Strauss hums a popular Christmas melody, and in the dim light we smile our secret smiles as the car moves forward in the snow-studded night.

THE ENGINEER

On the flight to Boston, Mitch thinks about his last visit home. "The next time I see you, Pop, I'll be wearing a uniform," he'd told his father. "I'll be a captain in the Air Force. Remember how I used to play soldier wearing your old uniform?" The old man, afflicted by a stroke that had deprived him of normal means of communicating, had only been able to twitch involuntarily. As a physician used to dealing with bedridden mutes, Mitch felt he should have been able to carry on a one-sided conversation, but the strain of trying to elicit a response had worn him down. He'd watched with distaste as soured milk spilled from his father's mouth and soiled the pillow. "Are you warm enough? It's in the seventies today, supposed to hit eighty tomorrow." When it was time to go, he'd felt the pressure of tears. "See you, Pop," he whispered.

His father hiccuped. "Las' time he had de hiccups, de doctah come an' give him a shot a somethin'," the home health aide commented cheerfully. "You know what dat doctah say? He say yo daddy's in good shape 'cept fo' his strokes. He say yo daddy prob'ly gonna live fo'evah!" The thought of his father going on and on like this was more than he could bear, but what did this Haitian girl care, although she'd probably seen more misery than most girls her age and should know better than to make light of the situation. Mitch wished she wouldn't smile so much.

Now, two weeks before Christmas, he's flying home at the request of his mother and sister, who've finally agreed to place his father in a nursing home but want him to be the one to break the news. They also want him to ride in the ambulance. "We'll just feel better knowing you're with him on the trip," his sister had said, but Mitch feels they've backed him into a corner. He's been dreading the trip for weeks.

When Dottie picks him up at Logan, he hardly recognizes her. Although it's been only six months since he last saw her, she looks older and fatter. She's gotten her graying hair butched and is wearing a puffy down jacket that accentuates her heavy arms and large bosom. His sister is in her early forties, four years his senior, but she looks fifty. If he thinks back far enough, he can remember a pretty, petite teenager who liked to dance, but he finds it difficult to connect that person with the person his sister has become.

"You'll have to tell Daddy tonight," she says as they walk to her van. Mitch is relieved to find the vehicle empty. Usually there are several yapping spaniels on board, but today there's only the pungent aroma of flea shampoo and tufts of honey-colored hair on the upholstery to remind him that his sister raises dogs to compensate for the children she's never had. "The ambulance is coming first thing tomorrow. I told them you're a doctor, so they're going to let you ride in the back with him."

Mitch grimaces. It's been threatening to snow since they left the airport, and now a steady veil of sleet obscures their vision. A car in front skids and swings sideways across the road. He tenses as Dottie applies the brakes. She'd always been a competent driver, so why is he so nervous? Ah, yes. He's gotten used to driving in the South, where it rarely snows. "Did I startle you?" she asks, reaching over to touch his knee reassuringly. "I'm sorry. See? Everything's fine now. You can relax, baby bro."

"Sorry," he mumbles sheepishly as they pull into the driveway of their parents' house in Newton. He can see their mother standing at the living room window watching for them. When he was in grade school, she'd be waiting for him in that window every afternoon. Who knew what evil might befall an eight-year-old who rode his bike?

Dorothy leans across the seat and whispers, "I'm not coming in."

"*What?*"

"She'll understand. Call me tomorrow, after the trip. Phil will meet you at the nursing home, give you a ride back."

Great. It was going to be a hard enough day without having to make conversation with his brother-in-law, whom he disliked.

"I can't believe I didn't tell you I wouldn't be staying."

He can feel his anger rising. "Well, you didn't." Damn her anyway.

"Forgive me. I'm at sixes and sevens these days."

He sighs. "Yeah, well. I guess it's been hard on everyone."

"You have no idea." Oh yes he does, but there's no use trying to ease her out of her martyrdom. And besides, she's the one who has to deal with their parents on a day-to-day basis, while he (and he can't help but guess how she's badmouthed him to all her friends) uses his peacetime commission as an excuse to remove himself from the situation. At any rate, he thinks bitterly, that's how *she* sees it. "I'll just be glad when tomorrow is over," she says. "Go on in, Mitch. She's waiting for you. She's been cooking for two days." She squeezes his hand and for the first time since she picked him up, he feels some of the warmth they'd shared as children.

He gets out of the van, stands beside the driveway, and watches her back out, turn onto the street, and head down the block—a familiar route. Years ago—too many years, it seems to him now—they'd been close enough to share a car, but recent circumstances had forced them apart. For instance, he'd been confused by her reluctance to move their father into a nursing home. Even after he'd carefully pointed out the advantages of total care, she'd flung her resistance at him like a spear, wounding him by her apparent disregard for their mother's mental and physical well-being. "Don't you care about her?" he'd shouted. "Don't you see what taking care of him is doing to her?" But Dorothy had remained obdurate, refuting him with stubborn silence. She'd taken a year to come around. Finally, they'd joined forces to convince their mother it was the proper thing to do.

"Mitchell." His mother, a small, round woman with thinning gray hair pulled back in a bun, hugs him tightly, and he can smell his childhood in her embrace.

"Dottie couldn't stay, Ma. Early supper for Phil—something like that." He feels obliged to cover for his sister, to protect his mother from further hurt. "It's good to be here," he lies as he looks around, thinking, *Everything is the same, it's always the same.* Take the aluminum tray he made her in Cub Scouts; it still sits on the coffee table, its design crudely etched into the metal—a rose with petals falling, the inspiration of a den mother who dabbled in art.

"This is very hard on Dottie," his mother says seriously. "You know how devoted she is to your father."

And I'm not? The implication hung in the air. Go ahead, say it, he wants to blurt, feeling a sudden rush of jealousy, Phil is the one Pop preferred. Two years before Mitch's graduation from medical school and one year before his father's first stroke, Dottie had brought Phil home and he'd been received like a natural son, the pal his father had always longed for, a down-to-earth, hardworking Joe he could talk business with, who'd help him knock off a six-pack while they watched the Celtics complete a championship season. "The hermit is upstairs with his books," Mitch overheard his father say when he was home studying for his boards and the rest of the family was gathered around the TV.

It hadn't always been like that. When he was small, his father, treasurer of a chain of women's clothing stores, had taken him on long business forays out into the suburbs to check on accounts. "This is my boy, Mitch," his father would say proudly when introducing him to the managers. Sometimes he'd been left to wander through the stores while his father handled business matters. He remembered watching the customers admiring themselves in the three-way mirrors, each woman a replica of his mother in some small way—the thrust of a hip, a toss of the head, the wave of a hand. Sometimes the saleswomen would recognize him. They'd offer him candy, too-sweet butterscotch squares that stuck to their cellophane wrappers like glue.

He puts his gear in his old room, where a framed lithograph of the *Bounty* still hangs. As a boy he dreamed of sailing around the world in such a ship. His mother follows him and stands beside the maple headboard that bears the scars of his childhood rage—once, when he'd been sent to his room as punishment for some act of defiance, he'd taken his mother's sewing scissors and carved his initials. Now he watches her as she traces the jagged letters with her fingers. "It wasn't like you," she says softly. "And afterward, when you realized what you'd done, you cried like a baby." Turning to face him, she adds, "I had to talk your father out of spanking you silly. Well. I don't guess you remember *that*." She wipes her hands on her apron. "As they say, that was then, this is now. Is there anything I can do to help you settle in?"

He smiles. "I'm supposed to be helping *you*, remember?"

She sighs. "I can't bear the thought of leaving this house."

"Why not stay?"

"By myself?"

"You've been by yourself for a year now," he replies, nodding in the direction of his father's room. "Pop's no company, that's for sure. Besides, you two had a pact. If anything happened to one of you, the other would stay on in the house. Do I have it right?"

She twists her hands together, a gesture, Mitch reminds himself, that Dottie has appropriated. "Well, if we ever *did* say that, and I'm not at all sure we did—where did you get such an idea, anyway?—we must have been out of our minds. Because this place is much too big for one person. Much, much too big."

"You could close off some rooms."

"Dorothy doesn't think that would be practical. Anyway, she

needs my help. You've no idea how busy she is, running off to shows, taking the dogs to vets. I could help her keep things tidy at home. Make dinner." She smiles. "Phil's not one to pitch in, you know."

He doesn't like picturing her in the role of housekeeper, with Dottie issuing orders and Phil sitting around doing nothing, but she seems willing enough. Still, he feels there are alternatives. "You could get an apartment in a retirement complex. You know, like your friend Hazel."

"I'd never be happy in a place like that! I'd rather be with family."

"Well, if that's what you really want, Ma." He sits down on his old bed, suddenly weary. What *he* really wants is a chance to be alone, to sort out his feelings. And, more than anything, he wants to change into civilian clothes—jeans, a sweatshirt, sneakers.

"Don't you want to put away your things? Here, let me help you," she says, opening a drawer in the dresser and lifting a shirt from his bag. "You haven't told me about Margaret and the girls. Do they like it in Louisiana? There." She smooths his folded underwear and places it in the second drawer with his socks. "It's silly not to unpack, Mitchell. After all, you're not leaving until Friday."

He knows this is not so much a reaffirmation as a plea: She wants, *needs* him to stay on and see her through the first rough days of solitude. "I've got to be back Wednesday night, Ma. Sorry. I meant to tell you that on the phone. I'm on call Wednesday night, and I couldn't get anyone to switch with me. And Margaret's counting on me getting back then, to help with the girls. You know how kids are around the holidays. They're ready to explode."

"I know. Of *course* I know," she says bravely. "Well. At least we'll have tonight, and tomorrow night, after you get back from the . . ." She stops herself from saying *nursing home*. He senses it's still a foreign phrase in her vocabulary, one that will have to be assimilated slowly into her everyday speech. *My husband is in a nursing home,* he imagines her telling the women in her sewing circle at the Episcopal church. They'll know how hard it is for her to talk about it. Mostly widows of men who've died of lingering illnesses, they'll understand. "You won't have to leave first thing in the morning, will you?" she asks, her voice buoyed with hope.

"My plane doesn't leave until three forty-five." He knows the hours will crawl the way they always do when he's home, but he feels obligated to make the best of it. Especially this time. "We'll have plenty of time to visit," he reassures her.

"Good," she says with a sigh. "Now. How about some lunch? I've made soup. You used to love my fish chowder. A big bowl, with some soda crackers on the side? That sound good?"

"Anything, Ma. I'm hungry. Been up since four this morning."

"He knows we're sending him away," his mother says. They are sitting in the kitchen at the small table where Mitch ate breakfast every morning of his life until he went away to college. He looks down at his chowder. Chunks of haddock, potatoes, and onions swirl around in the thick creamy broth he stirs with a bent-handled spoon, the spoon his mother always gives him when he comes home to visit. He has no idea how the handle got bent, but he can guess she could tell him. "You're imagining things, Ma. How could Pop know? Even if someone has told him, how would you know he knows? He doesn't emote. Or has there been some change?"

"There's been no change."

"Then you're projecting."

"I'm telling you, he *knows*. He saw me putting his pajamas in a suitcase. I tried to do it quietly, when he was asleep, but I had to get the suitcase down from his closet shelf, and when I turned around, his eyes were open. I had a feeling he was watching me the whole time. I knew I should have said something then, but I couldn't." She reaches for a Kleenex and dabs at her eyes. "That isn't quite true. I *did* say something. I *had* to, to cover up. I said I was taking the pajamas to a tailor to have them altered because he'd lost so much weight. Now isn't that silly? I mean, why would I put them in a suitcase, and why would I take them to a tailor? I'd fix them myself, like always. But no, I had to lie" She makes a sound that's halfway between laughter and tears. "Do you think that's awful?"

The hot chowder burns his throat as he swallows. "You did what you felt you had to, Ma. Sometimes it's necessary to tell little lies. There have been times when I've—when I thought it was in a patient's best interest not to hear the whole truth."

She reaches across the table to touch his hands. "Thank God you're here, Mitch. I feel better now that you're here."

"Did you say something about wanting me to help you sort some things in the attic?" he asks her. They've been sitting in front of the television where she's been watching her soap and he's been leafing through the one magazine his mother still gets, a review of the week's news and current affairs.

"You never told me what you wanted me to do with your train set," she says, without moving her head. Mitch knows she's been watching this particular program for years and can't bear to miss a minute.

"I said to keep it for the girls, remember? You asked me at Thanksgiving when I called, and I told you."

"Ah, so you did. I'm sorry. I forgot. I guess I have it in my mind that girls don't play with trains."

"These days girls *do* play with trains," he mutters, still sensitive about not having fathered a son.

"Well, I'll have to ship that stuff to you, because I won't be able to take it to Dorothy's."

"Jesus, Ma. Dottie and Phil have that whole barn! Can't they store some stuff for you in there? If you're afraid to ask, I will. Tomorrow, when I see him. Thing is, we just don't have room to store anything."

"I thought you said you had a house."

"Well, yes. Half a house. A duplex, I guess you'd call it. But we only have one small storage shed, and that's full of baby things." He might as well be talking to himself, he thinks, because the commercials are over and his mother is once again immersed in her program. He'll just have to go up to the attic himself and start sorting. What about the layout, the one he and his father had built using one big sheet of plywood that they split, painted, and hinged? They'd glued the tracks onto it, and afterward they'd added plaster of paris mountains, toothpick trees, and matchbox houses. It was one of the few times they worked together on a project, and Mitch could still recall the feeling of closeness they shared and their excitement when everything worked the way they wanted it to. His father had manned the switches at first. Then, noticing Mitch's eagerness, he'd said, "You be the engineer now, son. You be the one to make things go."

The attic smells of must and mothballs. He finds the layout beneath some boxes in a corner, marveling that it's still intact. His mother has already wrapped the trains in newspapers and placed them in liquor cartons, so all he has to do is take them down to the cellar, where, he hopes, Phil will pick them up.

This done, he joins her in the living room, where she's sitting on the couch looking at a scrapbook. "It's yours," she says, handing it to him. "I want you to have it. It's filled with everything you ever did in school."

He takes it from her and begins to turn the pages. "It's funny what you remember," he muses. "I used to spend a lot of time in my room studying and being teased about it by Pop." He wonders if she'll be startled by this recollection. Perhaps it hasn't occurred to her that he would harbor any unpleasant memories of his youth, but as he searches her face for any sign of distress, she turns away to fuss with some silk flowers in a vase.

"You haven't told me about those precious girls of yours," she says, pulling at the multicolored petals and stretching the leaves to fill the spaces between the wire stems. "I wish you weren't so far away."

After supper he goes into his father's room and sits beside the bed. The house is quiet except for the gentle click of the dishwasher and the furnace's low drone. His father's cheeks are flushed with the effort of passing a stool, and a ripe, noxious odor fills the room. Mitch cracks the window and watches as a brisk early-winter wind blows the curtains. When he touches his father's forehead, he is surprised at how soft the old skin feels. "I've something to tell you, Pop."

His father lies motionless, a shell waiting to be tossed by waves. Mitch knows there's a shred of intellect left inside that shell; he's observed too many patients in a similar condition to doubt this. He picks up a wash basin from beneath the bed and takes it into the bathroom, where he runs warm water, adding soap and a washcloth. Pulling back the sheet, he sponges his father's soft skin, skin as delicate as parchment. "It's not a bad place. You'll see, Pop. They'll take good care of you. It's not like a hospital. I know how you hate hospitals. You'll have a room of your own—" and here Mitch pauses because he doesn't know if the facility even has private rooms—"with curtains on the window, and TV." His father used to have the television on a lot, or was it the aides who liked to watch around the clock? Mitch can't recall. Now the screen is blank all the time, and his father seems not to care.

He dries his father's atrophied genitals and dusts them with powder, as he has seen his mother do, then plucks a fresh disposable diaper from the box beside the bed. "Ma feels bad about selling the house, but she thinks she'll be happy at Dottie's." He takes a clean pair of pajamas from the bureau, noting the now empty drawer. "You won't have to go in the ambulance alone, Pop." He lifts his father's brittle shoulders and eases the old man's withered arms into the sleeves, then buttons the jacket. "I'm going to ride with you." A tear forms in the corner of his father's left eye, trembles slightly, then slides across the bridge of his nose into the other eye before Mitch can blot it with a tissue. "There's nothing to be afraid of," he tells his father and himself. In the half-darkened room he thinks he hears his father sigh.

An early snow falls lightly in the wintry twilight as Mitch slips on his father's galoshes and overcoat, preparing to walk in the field behind his parents' house. Flakes stick to the branches of the tall pines and sink into the lumpy canvas of frosty grass. By tomorrow he guesses there'll be an accumulation of several inches. He'll have to call home and tell the girls; they've never seen a significant snowfall. As he walks, wet flakes stick to his hair and face and slide down his neck, reminding him of winters past. By morning the snow will lie heaviest on the top branches of the biggest trees, weighing them down until they look like old men praying, feathered druids who watch over the sleepers beneath the ground—hibernating animals, the dead who lie in cemeteries.

Back at the house, he remembers how his mother used to make him stand outside the back porch and pick balls of snow from his mittens, and when he looks up, she is there still telling him what to do. "Stamp your feet on the mat, dear. You can leave your father's galoshes in the laundry room to dry."As he peels off the worn overshoes, he senses the snow is already obscuring his footprints. Soon, in the diminishing light, his crooked tracks will be barely visible.

By the time his plane touches down in Shreveport, Mitch is yearning to see his wife and daughters. In the waiting area his arms ache from the happy burden of gifts his mother pressed upon him, boxes of various sizes whose strings cut into the skin at his wrists. When he bends to kiss the girls, he notices that their fine, wispy blond hair smells of chlorine from the officers' club pool. "Are all these presents really for us, Daddy?" the older one wants to know, her voice high-pitched and her eyes shining with excitement.

Margaret leans over the boxes to kiss him warmly. "We've missed you," she says, and the sound of her soft voice makes his heart skip a beat. She's wearing some new perfume whose sweet, floral scent reminds him of a spring meadow splashed with sunshine. In her presence, the sad events of the past few days begin to fade. Soon he'll be lost in the dizzy preparations for Christmas Eve, when his in-laws are scheduled to arrive. As for his mother, she'll be all right, he feels. She'll get caught up in Dottie and Phil's busy holiday schedule, and there'll be frequent visits to the nursing home, where the staff has promised to help her adjust. But what will become of his father, who now lies imprisoned in a sterile, unfamiliar room, cared for by strangers, with a roommate who calls out for someone named Mona? When Margaret asks, "Did everything go okay, Mitch?" he can only nod. "Of course it did," she says. "You're a good son. You did what you were supposed to do." She was right, he knew. Now it would be up to him to put it all behind him, to get on with the business of being jolly. This, too, was expected of him in the holiday season.

KANGA AND ROO

As Mattie stood in the front doorway of her daughter's house in Denver, she remembered the tiny baby, gray-blue from lack of oxygen, that the nurses had held up for her to see. It started then, her need to protect Roo from everything. And now she, Kanga (as Clifton had christened her, along with Roo, whose real name was Katherine,) was here to help her daughter, who was laid up with a ski injury. Roo's divorce had gone through the month before, and she had custody of the boy. Well, Mattie would do what she could. Wasn't that what mothers were supposed to do?

The cabbie carried her suitcase up the steep flight of stairs and onto the porch, where he waited for her to fish in her purse for the money to pay him. "I don't charge extra for the luggage," he said.

"You charge enough," Mattie said briskly as she handed him his fare, plus a modest tip. "Or is it because you think I'm a tourist? A skier?"

"You don't look like a skier," the young man said, eyeing the surplus. "And don't blame me. I don't set the rates. The company does."

She watched him run down the stairs and out to his cab, an older model with faded paint and dented fenders, before she tried the front door. It was ajar, so she pushed it open with her suitcase. "Roo? I'm here, hon," she called timidly.

Roo lay on the couch with her left leg, encased in a large brace that went from the sole of her foot to the top of her thigh, propped up on pillows. "Get a look at Robot Leg," she said. "Kids are scared shitless. It's the cogs that get them. They think I'm some kind of bionic woman. Christ! Am I glad to see you!"

As they embraced awkwardly, Mattie felt Roo's frail shoulders tremble, and marveled at her daughter's girlish appearance. At twenty-five, with her shoulder-length blond hair pulled back into a ponytail, she could still pass for a teenager. The stresses of single parenthood and a painful injury hadn't changed that. "Well," Mattie said, peeling off her coat and laying it across the back of the couch. "You're certainly fearless. I mean, the way you threw yourself down that slope. I heard all about it from Toady, you know. He gave me a blow-by-blow over the phone." Toady was Roo's five-year-old son. Roo's ex-husband, Ted, was a building contractor in Evergreen. It was he who'd come up with the nickname Toady. He said the kid swam like a frog, but that no kid should be called Froggy. (Toady and Roo had been swimming at the Y since he turned fifteen months.) Toady would be, Roo predicted, a star in the competitive swim program just as soon as he was old enough to race. She pointed out, matter-of-factly, that he'd inherited his agility from his father. Mattie remembered this, wondering why Roo didn't hate Ted's guts; after all, he *was* a womanizing son of a bitch, as Clifton said.

"Where's Toady now?" Mattie asked. "In school?"

Roo nodded. "Cal is picking him up. They should be here soon. He's *so* excited about seeing you! Did I mention you two will be bunking together? He can't wait to have you read him six bedtime stories." She pulled herself up to a sitting position, and winced with the effort.

"Does it hurt a lot?"

Roo grinned. "Only when I laugh. Hey. You want to unpack? Wash up? I'll take you downstairs." She reached for her crutches. "Yes, I can do stairs. Wait till you see. I'm a regular speed racer."

Mattie followed her through the kitchen and down a short flight of stairs that led to a bottom floor, really a converted basement. As she recalled from photographs, Roo and Toady had adjoining bedrooms at the end of a little hall, next to the bathroom. Another woman—was her name Cal?—had the other room downstairs. Mattie took an instant dislike to the dark hallway and the musty odor that hung in the air, but chided herself for doing so. What did she expect? It was, after all, a basement. "Here we are," Roo said, flicking the light switch to reveal a small bedroom with twin beds and scattered toys, obviously Toady's lair. "Sorry about the mess," Roo said. "Toady's pal Bud spent the night last weekend." Standing in the doorway, Mattie thought the room was too small for two beds, and she longed for a window. "The closet's in the hall, and the bathroom's across from Cal's room."

Mattie looked up and down the hallway and could only see one other door. "Where do *you* sleep?" she asked.

"Now, Mom, I don't want you to get upset, but Toady and I share this room, except when he has a pal over. Then I bunk with Cal. Like now."

Mattie made a face.

Roo sighed. "I *told* Cal you wouldn't approve. Let me explain it this way: by taking the smaller room, we save twenty bucks a month. Get it?"

Mattie looked at her watch. In less than a half hour she'd succeeded in raising Roo's hackles. Well, Clifton had warned her. *Be prepared,* he'd said. *She'll be defensive.* How well he knew his daughter. "So," Mattie continued, taking a deep breath and digging in. "This Cal is your tenant?"

"Mm-hm. And a close friend. Oh, Mom. I knew you'd get upset."

"I'm not upset. It's just that, well, I'm surprised. I guess I expected things were going better for you. You haven't asked us for money recently. What is it, honey? Ted not keeping up with his payments?"

Roo lifted Mattie's suitcase onto a bed and unzipped it. "That shouldn't come as any great shock."

Mattie realized she'd hit a nerve. Of course Roo would be sensitive about Ted. She might even still care for him, now that some time had passed and she'd had months to sort out her feelings. Should she apologize for mentioning his name? She couldn't decide. Instead, she stood by and watched Roo unpack her things, piling sweaters, putting cosmetics on the bureau next to Toady's first-grade photo with its cocky, sweet expression. Mattie longed for Toady, who'd surely provide a welcome buffer. When did school let out, anyway? It was already after three.

"I see you came prepared for cold weather," Roo observed. "You won't be needing all these woolens, you know. Denver's really quite mild in midwinter."

Annoyed, Mattie felt like saying she wished Roo had told her about the climate. Instead, she watched her sweaters being jammed into a drawer. "Here. Let me do that," she said. "You shouldn't be waiting on me. You should be putting your leg up."

They sat opposite each other at the small dining room table, Roo opening her mail, Mattie sipping chamomile tea from a mug that read, THE BEST MAN FOR A JOB IS A WOMAN. Looking out the picture window, she observed streets cleared of the snow that had fallen just a week ago (at least a foot of snow, according to Roo). Now only a few dirty clumps remained. At least Mattie could console herself with Roo's selection of a good, solidly middle-class neighborhood, judging by the appearance of neat front porches and fenced-in yards. Across the way, Mattie could see into a living room where an older man and woman were drinking from saucered cups, a nice old-fashioned touch. A television screen flickered in the background, probably Oprah. Back home in New Hampshire the dog would be itching to go out. She hoped her neighbor remembered, because Clifton wouldn't be home from hospital rounds until after six.

Roo was sorting her mail, putting bills in one pile and junk flyers in another. When Mattie heard footsteps on the front porch she said out loud, "That must be Toady," and jumped up. She could feel her heart beating with excitement as she anticipated their reunion. She could already taste his skin, smell his hair. Six months had passed since she'd seen him. He'd be taller, and smarter, she knew.

"GramMAW!" he yelled as he bounded into the room, his lunchbox clattering to the floor.

"You *are* taller," Mattie said, pleased with his enthusiastic greeting. "I can't believe my eyes! You've changed so much."

"Mom," Roo interjected. "This is Cal."

Mattie disengaged herself from Toady's energetic hugging and stood up to face the tall, thin, bearded man who held out his hand. "Oh my," she said, shielding her face and laughing. "I thought—I mean . . ."

Cal smiled. "I know. I bet you thought Cal was short for Carolyn."

"Mom, I could swear I told you," Roo said, clearly embarrassed.

Both women watched him lope into the kitchen. Mattie heard the click and hiss of beer being opened. He came back with a bag of pretzels and two cans of Coors, one of which he offered Mattie.

"No, thanks," she said, putting up her hands. "I prefer wine."

"Oh, God," Roo moaned, rolling her eyes. "I forgot."

"As if you haven't had more important things to think about." Mattie could feel her face flushing, though she couldn't explain why. "Soda's fine, or even water. Do you have good-tasting city water? I should think so, this being the Rockies."

Cal chuckled. "Ah. Those mountain springs in the beer ads, right? Actually, though, our tap water isn't *too* bad." He gave Roo a beer and started back into the kitchen, then paused to ask, "Want ice with your water?"

"Please." Mattie couldn't take her eyes off Toady, who fidgeted self-consciously under her adoring gaze. "Come over here, honey bun," she said, patting a place on the couch. "Did Mommy tell you Grandpa's dying to take you fishing this summer? Wouldn't it be fun to fly back east all by yourself?"

He took a running leap backward and landed beside her, causing water to slosh on her skirt. "Jesus, yes!"

"Toady," Roo scolded. "Don't say *Jesus*. And watch what you're doing."

"Right!" said Cal, handing Mattie a Flintstones glass with water and ice cubes. "Simmer down, big guy."

"You say Jesus," Toady whined. "Why can't I?"

"Because it's not nice to swear."

"I thought Jesus was a good guy."

Cal nodded. "The best."

"Then why is it a bad thing to say his name?"

"I'm *very* thirsty," Mattie said, eager to change the subject. "Won't you help me get a Coke?"

"Coke is bad for you," Toady said, grinning.

"Not the kind that comes in a can and fizzes," Cal said, playfully poking Toady in the arm.

"Oh, yeah," Toady nodded. "Okay, Grammaw, I'll get you a Coke."

A modern kid in the know, Mattie mused as she watched him bounce across the room, talking about things he couldn't possibly understand. Or could he? She shifted her attention to Roo. "Shouldn't you be lying down on the couch, keeping your leg higher than your heart? To reduce the swelling?"

Roo looked at Cal. "You'd never know she was married to a doctor, would you?"

"I thought maybe she was a nurse," he replied, turning to Mattie. "My mother's an LPN. Sharp as a tack. Knows lots of things. Picks up bits and pieces from eavesdropping on the pros, I guess. When my sisters and I were growing up, we hardly ever saw a doctor."

Toady ran in with an open can of soda and dribbled some on the rug. "Uh-oh," he said, looking at his mother. "I'm in deep now!"

Mattie took the can from Toady's wet hands and blotted the drops with a piece of Kleenex she took from her pocket. "Anyone can have an accident," she reassured him before turning to Cal, curious about the stranger who seemed to be taking over her daughter's life. "Where are you from? I mean, originally?"

"Born in Oregon, near Portland," he responded, cradling his beer in big, callused hands that looked accustomed to hard work. "Stayed there pretty much all my growing-up years. After high school, I did the community college bit. Dropped out after a year of boring classes. Then I went out to Spokane and worked there awhile. Been in Denver for three years." He sipped the last of his beer, then squashed the can and handed it to Toady. "Here, pilgrim."

"I'm not a pilgrim," replied Toady sullenly.

"Well, then, buddy. Are you my buddy?"

"Yeah," Toady mumbled. "I guess so."

"Then do me a favor and toss this into the recycling bin. And bring me another from the fridge. Okay?"

Toady walked slowly into the kitchen, scuffing his heels. It was obvious to Mattie that he harbored some ambivalent feelings toward Cal, but that, at the same time, he was trying to please. Wasn't that what any six-year-old would try to do?

"Well," Cal drawled, "where was I? Oh, yeah. Denver. Moved in here with your daughter about four months ago. Before that I was living in a real dump. Then suddenly it seemed like time to upgrade, if you know what I mean."

Mattie nodded, thinking he seemed like an okay guy, down-to-earth, who'd grown fond of Roo and Toady. Not an opportunist. Besides, what did Roo have to offer him other than affection and affordable shelter? As a single mom, she had her own problems. Mattie just wished she'd known about their involvement sooner.

Roo moved to the couch and was using the remote to channel-surf for news, causing faces to fly by at a dizzying pace. At home it would be seven o'clock, and the evening meal, prepared by Mattie and left in the freezer, would be microwaved and ready for Clifton to eat once he had finished his bourbon and water. Mattie wondered what Roo had planned for dinner, but felt shy about asking. She wanted to help. Wasn't that why she'd flown all the way out here?

Toady held out a bag of potato chips. "Want one?" he asked her. "These are *awesome*."

"Don't spoil your appetite," Mattie said, moving Roo's beer from its puddle on the coffee table onto a newspaper, where it could sweat without damaging the finish.

"Impossible!" Cal said. "The kid's a bottomless pit."

Toady laughed. "You got *that* right."

"Cal is going to make nachos," Roo announced. "He makes the best nachos in all of Denver. Just dripping with cheese."

They had nachos, and drumsticks rolled in Mexican-spiced bread crumbs, and a salad of avocado, sliced onion, and shredded lettuce. "This is delicious!" Mattie said. "Where'd you learn to cook like this?"

"Didn't Roo tell you? I work as a chef at The Natural Choice. Or I did work there. Now I'm working for the Food Service at DU. Not nearly as much fun, but the university benefits are good. Gotta have those benefits, huh, Roo?" he said, winking.

Mattie guessed they were inching toward a commitment but, knowing Roo was still gun-shy, she wasn't sure exactly what kind. She intended to query Roo when Toady wasn't around. He'd eaten with gusto, then gotten quiet. Too much grown-up conversation, she guessed. Wanting to include him, she patted her lap. "Remember when you used to cuddle with me? Come here and let me give you a hug."

He sat up straight, a shift in posture that told her he meant business. "I don't feel like smooching right now," he declared.

"Who said anything about smooching? I promise I won't kiss you."

"Honest?" He regarded her warily. "You always want to."

"You used to like it. I remember when you couldn't get enough kisses."

"Well, I'm too big for that mushy stuff now."

"Oh," she said, feeling genuinely sad at the passage of time. "That's really too bad. I guess you're growing up."

Roo ruffled Toady's hair with her hand. "He likes to think so. Hey. Wanna help Cal with the dishes? Then maybe Gram will let you give her a bath."

Toady giggled and became a little boy again, much to Mattie's relief. "What's so funny?" she asked, playing along. "I need someone to wash my back."

"Daddy washes Coral's back," he said soberly, picking up an empty platter and walking carefully to the kitchen. "She likes it."

When he was out of sight, Mattie whispered to Roo, "Who's Coral?"

Roo sighed. "Ted's latest bimbo. She's living with him now, I think. At least that's what Toady says. Apparently, she's in for the long haul. Or thinks she is."

At first Mattie had tried to defend Ted, suggesting maybe Roo was wrong about his infidelities, but Clifton told her she was crazy. "A guy that good-looking, and a cocky son of a bitch to boot. I could have told you it wouldn't last," he said angrily. After the breakup, Mattie knew there was no use reminding Cliff it takes two to make a marriage work. She loved Roo to pieces, but she also knew her daughter wasn't perfect. Roo had been a willful little girl, and the trait remained. If only they'd waited to have a child until they were sure everything was going to work out. But then, Mattie reminded herself, there wouldn't have been Toady.

She remembered Ted and Roo and their wedding day. "Now that we're married, I'm not calling her Roo anymore," he'd announced. "I'm calling her Kiki. That's short for Katherine."

Cliff had laughed. "What's Roo think of this? She's had her nickname since she was a baby."

"Oh, she'll do anything I say. She's crazy about me. Hasn't she told you, Pop?"

"I hate it when he calls me Pop," Cliff said that night, already predicting trouble.

"Toady spend much time with his dad?" Mattie asked when the table had been cleared and Roo was settled on the couch with her leg propped up on pillows. The noisy kitchen cleanup, punctuated by loud hijinks, continued.

"A weekend a month and holidays, except for Christmas."

"Oh God. What'll we do about July Fourth? That's when we planned to have him with *us*."

Roo winced. "Can we please not deal with that shit right now? My leg is killing me."

While Toady got ready for bed, Mattie finished unpacking. She piled the rest of her clothing at the foot of the bed, not wanting to create more upheaval than was absolutely necessary. Roo and Cal were upstairs watching television; she had used settling in as an excuse to give them some privacy. Toady, dressed in baseball-player pajamas, sat cross-legged on his bed, watching her. "Do you want me to read you a story?" she asked him. "You can pick your favorite."

He yawned and slid beneath the covers. "Not tonight. I'm too tired."

She sat on the edge of his bed and kissed his forehead. "Not too big for a smooch goodnight, I hope."

He shook his head.

"Good. I like that."

He sighed and turned on his side. "Turn off the light, please, Grammaw."

"I'll try not to wake you when I come to bed."

"Mom says I sleep like a rock. What do rocks sleep like?"

"Like you, I guess." She patted his back, rubbing the slender shoulder blades he'd inherited from his mom. She remembered all the times she'd tucked Roo in. Toady lay still, eyes shut, pretending to be asleep. *Funny he won't let himself go with me,* she thought. *Even though I know he's excited to have me sharing his room.*

She left the door ajar so that a sliver of light would save him from the dark. Roo always had to have a night light, the kind with the little plastic shade you flip off when you change the bulb. There was no night light in Toady's room. Mattie wondered if they kept each other from being afraid.

On Saturday Mattie and Toady went to the Natural History Museum. "He's crazy about geology," Roo told her. "You'll have to pry him away from all those boring rocks."

"Do you know they used to mine gold near here?" Toady asked, when they'd spent twenty minutes looking at agates. "In Cripple Creek. Cal says he's going to take me up there some time. You can ride on a little train and see just where they took the gold out of the ground."

"That would be fun," she responded, trying to sound enthusiastic. She'd awakened with a headache, a sign that usually meant she was coming down with a bad head cold or some pesky virus. Whatever it was, she hoped it would be short-lived. She fished in her purse for a small pill container that held Tylenol. "Honey bunch, Gram's going to get a drink of water," she said. "Stay right here till I get back." Toady nodded dreamily, his attention directed at an array of polished agates that shone like jewels against black velvet cushions. Mattie realized that the contrast between the darkness of the room and the brilliantly lit display cases only served to increase her discomfort. She also realized she could have avoided the museum trip entirely if Roo had stuck to the original plans. Technically, it was Ted's weekend to take Toady, but that arrangement had been altered because Mattie was visiting. Roo had decided to invite Ted over for Sunday dinner. She informed Mattie that Coral and Cal would be there, too. The potentials for disaster mounted, making Mattie's head pound even more. Earlier, Toady had remarked that Coral was a ditz brain. Mattie could imagine Ted being happy with such a person, someone who'd never challenge him.

When she returned to the agate display, Toady wasn't there. "Have you seen a little boy with blond hair and a blue jacket?" she asked a security guard, chiding herself for leaving Toady for three minutes. Roo would be furious.

The guard pointed at an archway that led into another room. "You mean that kid over there?" he asked.

"Toady!" she yelled, relief superimposing itself on the headache. "Didn't I ask you to wait for me?"

"You gotta be careful these days," the guard warned Toady. "You never know who's hanging around, waiting to snatch kids."

"I only went around the corner to see the dinosaurs," Toady said, his voice barely audible. "I'm sorry."

"Didn't I tell you we'd go there next?" Mattie was conscious of the irritation in her voice. "You should have waited for me to get back." Toady looked contrite and on the verge of tears. "Oh, honey," she said, feeling sorry for him and wanting to lighten his mood. "Should we stop at the gift shop on our way out?"

Toady brightened. "Can we?"

"Thank you," Mattie said to the guard, who was walking into the next room and seemed not to hear. She guessed he was used to grateful, careless grandmothers.

Roo and Mattie were waiting for Cal to get home from work. He was stopping to pick up Chinese so nobody would have to fuss. Toady was downstairs playing with the *T. rex* Mattie had bought him in the gift shop. "Feeling better, Mom?"

"Yes, thank God. My headache's gone."

"Sometimes it's the altitude." Roo was lying on the floor exercising: one hundred leg lifts, then a brief rest before the next set, to the thumping rhythms of rock music. "I wonder how long it'll be before I can get back to work," she shouted. It suddenly dawned on Mattie that she didn't know whether Roo was still working part time as a secretary in the graduate school of business. "I'll probably have to wait until I can really walk well because of carrying the heavy trays, huh?"

"So," Mattie said, lowering the volume on the stereo. "You're back to waiting tables. What happened to the secretarial job?"

"I can make more money waiting tables at The Natural Choice."

"Isn't that where . . ."

"Uh-huh. That's how I met him. But that's not the only reason I took the job. The food is very wholesome. The management's great. They're very picky about who they hire. I wouldn't wait tables just anywhere."

Mattie guessed this last statement was meant to reassure her but thought, with dismay, how disappointed Cliff would be. His darling Roo a waitress. The divorce was bad enough, but Cliff had hoped Roo would come to her senses and return to college. Mattie tried to prepare him. She knew Roo was certainly bright enough, but lacked the motivation to continue her studies. Mattie managed to say, "Well, honey, as long as you're happy." Privately, she wondered how Roo and Toady were managing. No mention had been made of another loan. Perhaps that issue would be raised in the few days remaining. Naturally, Cliff would agree to send her whatever she needed, but Mattie wished Roo would just come out with the request. Now she'd have to spend the rest of her visit worrying, wondering when it would come up in conversation, or if. "I guess waiting tables can be lucrative," she said, wanting to broach the subject but being too timid to do so.

Roo paused in her efforts to take a pull of water from the plastic bottle she kept at her side. "*Lucrative*. That's a *Daddy* word. What're you doing with a word like that, Mom?"

Mattie ignored the insult. She was suddenly overwhelmed with concerns. Would the headache return? How was Roo ever going to get her life back on track? Why couldn't she shake the feeling that she was in the way? Maybe she shouldn't have come.

Roo, reading her mother's distress, tried to make amends. "Oh, Mom," she said, pulling herself to a sitting position and reaching for Mattie's hands. "I was only kidding. I know how much you both worry about me. And I love you for it."

But it was too late. Mattie was dabbing at her cheeks with the corner of the apron she'd brought, knowing Roo wouldn't have one. "I . . . I can't imagine why I'm doing this," Mattie mumbled. Early on, she'd been critical of Roo's style of mothering. Why did it bother

her that Roo didn't hover over Toady? When he was an infant wailing away in his crib, Roo let him cry until his whole body shook with the effort. It seemed so heartless to Mattie, who could only remember being Kanga and wanting to keep Roo safe in her pouch forever. So when Clifton told her he'd checked with a colleague, a pediatrician, who confirmed that today's mothers seemed more detached from their infants, Mattie pretended to feel better.

She watched Roo exchange her water bottle for a diet soda. Wasn't there something about artificial sweeteners that was harmful when taken in large doses? It seemed to her that Roo was skinny and didn't need to worry about putting on weight. There'd been a time in high school when Mattie was convinced Roo was anorexic. Once she'd caught her sticking her finger down her throat to induce vomiting. The memory of that discovery made Mattie feel ill even now. There followed a few sessions of family counseling during which Mattie felt completely to blame. Then came a period of hostile silence, a barrier that remained until Ted came on the scene. Now, although she knew they'd long since established a pattern of mutual respect, she acknowledged the fragility of a truce that could be shattered by something so slight as a weighted glance.

As it turned out, Mattie's worries about Sunday dinner were needless, because Ted decided he wanted Toady to spend the day with him after all. Mattie watched the two of them approach Ted's little black Mazda and stood in the doorway until she'd made sure he'd fastened his son's seat belt. Disappointingly, Coral elected to remain in the passenger seat, her face shaded from view.

When Mattie offered to treat Roo and Cal to dinner, he suggested The Natural Choice, where she gamely ate brown rice and stir-fried veggies with tiny shrimp and cheerfully dipped her spoon into tofu ice cream, saying how much she enjoyed the meal, with all its unaccustomed textures and flavors. Mattie did notice how clean the place was, how fresh-faced and friendly the help seemed, how solicitous they were of Roo. These observations made her feel better about Roo's job as a waitress, though she knew Clifton wouldn't be as easily appeased. Mattie also knew it would be futile to insist that Roo, despite her lack of *achievements,* seemed happy. She felt certain Clifton wouldn't understand.

Cal wanted her opinion of the yogurt-honey dressing, which he said was his own concoction. Mattie smiled and said it was delicious, though secretly she would have preferred blue cheese. Sitting opposite them, with Roo's foot propped against her thigh, she felt comfortable about the particular direction her daughter's life was taking. She sipped her second glass of Chardonnay. This city of young people was beginning to win her over. She even felt younger herself. The thought of returning to New England in mud season soured her temporarily, until she recalled the promise of a late spring and the summer to follow, with Clifton taking her sailing on his days off, and lazy hours spent reading on the little sandy beach at the lake.

As she angled her way into the backseat of Cal's battered Saab, she realized that, after tonight, there'd be only one more chance for her to read Toady a bedtime story, to tuck him in snugly, to kiss him goodnight. As for plans to have him visit this summer, she felt they'd have to wait until Ted gave his approval.

Mattie and Cal decided it would be best if Roo didn't accompany them to the airport, but they included Toady, because he would have been heartbroken if they hadn't. Like most little boys, he loved planes. "When I come to visit, will I really fly all by myself?" he asked his grandmother as they waited for her to board. "Will I really sit next to someone I don't even know?"

"Yes," Mattie replied, smiling. "You will."

"Cool."

"Will you give me a hug before I get on the plane?"

"Sure."

She sensed he was anxious for her to go, not because he didn't love her, but because he wanted to get on with the next phase of his life, which involved some kind of day care arrangement after school now that Roo couldn't pick him up at three. She felt he was a little scared of this new adventure, but she trusted him to be cheerful and brave. He was, in her eyes, a most wonderful child, willing to be a good sport about practically everything.

"You know," he said seriously, "Dad and Coral are taking me to California this summer."

"I had heard that," Mattie said.

"And Mom and Cal are taking me camping."

"Yes. That'll be fun, won't it?"

"And you and Grampaw want me to come visit."

"That's our plan."

"Well," he sighed, "I only hope I can fit it all in."

For the first time, Mattie was aware of how complicated his life had become. How did it really feel to be five and be pulled in three different directions? "Look at me, Toady," she said, drawing him near and feeling him yield, then resist, then yield again. "We'll make sure you get to do everything. Don't you worry."

She could see by his even, open gaze that he trusted her to make things right. "Well, then," he said, sounding remarkably like his grandfather, "I guess things'll work out okay."

Long after the plane lifted into the sky, Mattie thought about her grandson's farewell. Toady had been sad when she left, which pleased her. Each time she saw him, she wanted to put him in her pocket and never let him go. The memory of being Kanga was still with her; sometimes she felt it had never left. Roo, though clearly an independent woman with a life completely her own, would always remain in need of protection. Perhaps Mattie had clung too tightly. Perhaps she'd never really been able to let go. If only there had been other children. Friends said it wasn't until your third or fourth child that you began to relax and enjoy parenthood. These same friends told her that being a grandmother was great: all the joys and none of the worries. *Not true,* Mattie thought. *Not true. I will worry about them both until I die.*

Clifton would probably agree. He would know what to say to her tonight as they ate their late supper in the kitchen, warmed by the radiant heat thrown out by the little coal stove. He'd want to know all the details of her visit, and she'd tell him just what she wanted him to know, leaving out the part about Ted's coming to snatch Toady away for a day. She would make Cal a neighbor instead of a companion. Nothing must be said to make Roo seem more vulnerable. Mattie would convince him that Roo was finally in control of her life, and that everything was going to be smooth sailing from now on. Perhaps when she saw that Clifton believed this, she would allow herself to believe it too.

SANCTUARY

Tess, my old college roommate and onetime best friend, she of the slim, wiry shape and the eyes that remind me always of ripe colossal olives, has put Kevin and me in separate rooms because she thinks we are no longer intimate, because she thinks I don't want to be physically close to someone who is dying of cancer. She says, ". . . because you will both rest better," but I know what she means. She means that she herself would not want to be in the same bed with him. I could argue, but why? Kevin, in his new mode, has accepted the arrangement, and so I am to sleep on the daybed in Tess's studio, where now, in the summer heat of a Santa Fe noon, everything shimmers. At night the street lamp outside the window above my bed casts interesting shadows on her easel and drawing board.

Last night I woke to the sound of Ermine the cat scratching in her box. Ermine doesn't like me and has implied that it's difficult for her to share the house, especially the studio, but that she'll tolerate me if I don't stay too long. When I tell Tess this she asks me when I learned cat talk. She says Ermine gets to like practically everybody eventually, so it's a shame we can't stay longer. I tell her we have to get back because of Kevin's precarious, uh, condition. He looks gaunt and waxen, and his clothes hang on him despite my efforts to purchase smaller sizes. "I like that cotton sweater you gave me for

Christmas," he said recently. "I *like* things that are roomy, remember?" His pale complexion, once ruddy, contrasts dramatically with the bold red of the sweater, a color I chose to cheer both of us. His hair, recently grown in past the stubble stage, now sticks straight up. My punk, skinny darling.

"Hey," he whispers to me. "I'll sneak into your bed tonight, while Tess is sleeping. That is, if she doesn't beat me to it."

"What are you saying?"

"Oh, come on, Laura. She's always had a thing for you. Then I came along and ruined everything."

"Will you stop?"

"I just can't believe you didn't know how she felt about you. It was so *obvious*."

"*Obviously* not. *I* didn't notice." He knows I'm lying; I can see it in his eyes. There were times when she'd touch my shoulder in a different way, to point out something, like a bird flying low on the horizon at sunset, or a child running in a playground. I knew, but pretended to myself I didn't. "Look, Kevin, I wish you'd said something. If I'd known you felt this way, I never would have pushed to take this trip. We could have gone on a cruise, rented a cottage on the Cape . . ."

At this moment Tess opens the French doors that lead out onto the patio and steps inside, carrying a tray of margaritas. "At your service," she says. "Remember Cancún, Laura? Oh no, you *wouldn't* remember. You got drunk every afternoon." She puts down the tray and turns to Kevin. "Spring break, junior year," she explains perfunctorily. "You were probably studying for GREs."

"Bottoms up," he says, licking salt from the rim of his glass. "Here's to good times gone by. Eh, Laura?"

Tess wants me to go running with her while Kevin is relaxing on the patio reading yesterday's paper, with Ermine sitting beside him feigning interest. Out on the dirt path that serves as a road we stretch, and I notice how limber she is. In the ten years since we graduated, she's hardly changed. If anything, she's thinner. She seems in perfect condition, whereas I can't even touch my forehead to my knees. "Look at me. I'm stiff as a board!" I complain. "I feel like an old lady."

"It's all that sitting around in hospitals," Tess says soothingly. "You can't help that. But soon . . ."

I put up my hand to stop her, and for a minute I think she will, but no, that wouldn't be Tess. She's got to spell it all out. "What I mean is, there must be times when you *wish* it was over. For his sake and well as yours." Her eyes lock with mine. "You can't deny that, can you?"

Before I can answer, she's off at a brisk pace and I'm left behind to consider my guilty response. She's right. I'd give anything to be free. For him to be free. But these are secrets I'm not supposed to divulge. Now if she were me, she'd spill them all out in confession, like the good Catholic she was raised to be.

When she realizes I'm not keeping up, she doubles back. "You could—come out here—and be with me," she says breathlessly. "Remember that—when the going—gets rough."

There are moments when I ask myself if I'll ever be happy again. Naturally, these are feelings I can't share with Kevin, so I keep pushing them back, avoiding any thoughts of the future. A friend has suggested I see a therapist, establish a rapport with someone now, so that when I really need the support, it'll be there. But I feel guilty thinking about myself when Kevin is the needy one. I don't feel like explaining this to Tess. I shouldn't have to, really. We've been out of touch with each other's lives for so long. How can she possibly know what it's like to see the one you love slip away?

Now, in tandem, we run along the crest of the hill in back of her house. I glance at Tess and wonder if she's as content as she pretends to be. She lives alone—by choice, apparently. Says she likes it that way. Says she gets more done on the weekends when her true watercolorist self takes over from the commercial artist. Judging from the number of finished canvases stacked in her studio, she keeps working even when she's supposed to be relaxing. I scan her face for signs of joy, but she's wearing her runner's mask, that countenance of agony and annoyance, so who can tell?

The city of Santa Fe sprawls below us on our right, and on our left, small dusky hills bunch. I admire the soft brown of the adobe houses and the spiked cedar fences, so different from the austere architecture of my native New England. Yes, I think I could be happy here, but I can't possibly commit to anything right now.

My calves begin to cramp, but I continue to push, feeling the need to prove there's nothing wrong with *me*. As if Kevin's disease was something I could catch, like measles or chicken pox.

Tess has gotten us tickets to see *The Magic Flute* despite her aversion to classical music. "Hate Mozart, love this place," she says, referring to the magnificent open-air setting. "Whenever I get bored, I just look up there." She indicates a sky that's heavy with a drama of its own as a new front moves in.

Throughout the performance, she fidgets on my left while Kevin, on my right, tenses his muscles in discomfort. Despite these distractions, I, who love Mozart, am transported by the music. Later, over drinks at a café behind the Governor's Palace, I tell Kevin and Tess dreamily, "The duet between Papagena and Pamina—wife and man, and man and wife—I could listen to it forever."

"Ooh, I dunno. Forever?" Tess giggles. "Forever's such a long, long time. Let's sing a few bars of that duet, see how it holds up."

"A few bars!" Kevin obliges loudly. He is drunk from a combination of painkillers and liquor. "Although I *do* like the part when the kids come out dressed as forest folk and wiggle their behinds at the audience. Now that's what I call *cute!*"

"Forest folk! I love it!" Tess guffaws.

Suddenly I feel like crying. What am I doing here with these insensitive jerks?

On the way back to Tess's house, Kevin and I sit like strangers in the backseat. After a while he says, "I'm sorry I made fun of your favorite song. If we were to get married all over again, I'd pay somebody to sing it at the ceremony."

His voice is soft and earnest, almost sober. "I love you," I say, not caring that he's just trying to please. His hands are warm and moist. Suddenly we're teenagers necking in the back of his parents' car. His tongue slips into my mouth, probes, insists that I respond in kind. It's been so long.

Tess turns up the radio. Rap chokes the air with angry epithets and thumping rhythms as she drives, too fast, through the darkness, leaving the small, sweet talk to us.

The next day is a scorcher, but sight-seeing is on the agenda, and realizing how eager Tess is to show us around, we acquiesce. By mid-afternoon the heat is making me so uncomfortable I want to scream, but she insists a particular foray will be worth the discomfort. Fifteen minutes outside of Santa Fe, riding in a car with a broken air conditioner, I am beginning to doubt it. Kevin is stretched out on the backseat, his knees drawn up to his chest. He's taken off his shirt and is using it for a pillow.

"He's asleep again," Tess notes. "Is that normal?"

I nod. "Pain meds'll do it. And the big lunch. He usually doesn't eat that much. Actually, with the heat and all, I feel kind of drowsy myself."

"Nap, then. Or don't you trust me to stay alert? Who was always the driver on our ski trips?" She taps her fingers lightly on the steering wheel, keeping time to the soundtrack from *The Big Chill,* a tape I'd sent her years ago because I loved the music, never dreaming that someday I'd be summoning Kevin's friends to mourn him, replicating the plot of the movie. Weren't we going to live forever? I can feel my throat thicken. Tears well. I half expect Tess to notice and say, "There you go again!" but instead she pulls off the highway onto a smaller road that slopes down into a valley. "You're gonna love this church," she says cheerfully. "I always bring visitors here. The *santuario* is a revelation, and the best part is, you don't even have to be Catholic to appreciate it."

As we pull into the sleepy village of Chimayo, Kevin wakes, sits up and stretches, pulls on his shirt, and leans forward. "Is this the famous shrine?" he asks. "Funny. I don't *feel* like a pilgrim. Give me a hand, will you, Laura, my sweet?"

I help him stand, supporting him gently by holding his waist. Tess is already out of the car, fiddling with her camera. The church, with its twin adobe towers topped by simple wooden crosses, looks anything but imposing. Around us, dogs lie napping in the afternoon dust and children play in the creek that runs through the square. "Here, you guys," she instructs us. "Get over there and I'll take your picture."

Kevin breaks away from my hold and reaches for the camera. "No, you two pose," he says. "My pinup days are over."

As Tess and I move together, our arms find each other's waists. "Say cheese," Kevin prompts. "Hey. You look the same as you did at graduation. Remember? Tess didn't want to take off her sunglasses."

Yeah, I remember. She'd been crying. Not surprising, since I'd just told her Kevin and I were getting married. Foolishly, I'd waited until minutes before the ceremony to break the news. She insisted on wearing those sunglasses so nobody would notice her swollen eyes. Everybody thought she was just being cool. "Christ, Laura!" she'd sobbed. "You've only known him a couple of months. Lots of people get engaged, then wait a year to see if it's right. And what am *I* supposed to do?" Her words come back to me now as I feel the pressure of her hand cupping my waist. "We were going to share that apartment in the city. Or have you forgotten?" Kevin's words come back to me: *She always had a thing for you.*

The picture taken, Tess pulls abruptly away. "I don't remember much about graduation," she says curtly, "except that god-awful restaurant where we waited hours to be served. My stepfather threatened to walk out without paying, the son of a bitch. Did I tell you he dropped dead last year? Coronary. He had it coming. Ah, well. Who gives a fuck? Come on. Let's go into the church and I'll give you the fifty-cent lecture." She gets on Kevin's other side and we make a chair with our hands. "Sit," she commands. He does, and we carry him inside. His shirt is soaked with sweat, but it's not from the heat. When you take enough drugs, I've learned, your clothing is always damp.

Inside the sanctuary, we sit on wooden chairs that teeter on uneven legs and listen to Tess, her voice low and reverent as she recounts the shrine's history. I wait for Kevin to make a smart remark. Instead, he's quiet and respectful, an attitude he's assumed, I guess, to please Tess, who seems to take all this very seriously. "You never told me she was a Catholic," he said the day before, when she got up early to go to Sunday mass.

I shrugged my shoulders. I'd always known that Tess prayed, and guessed that beneath that harsh exterior lurked a tender, trusting soul. Her own father, Boston Irish to the core, exerted a strong influence over her young life. I think she continued to emulate him after her parents divorced, just to spite her freethinking, nonchurchgoing mother. And later I'd assumed it was her spirituality that drew her to the Southwest.

In the chapel, people are praying and lighting candles. Tess points out a large, heavy cross leaning against one wall. "See that? A man carried it across the country as an act of penance in the hope his son would return home safely from 'Nam."

"And did he?"

"What do you think?" Before I can answer, she says, "Don't tell me. I want you to see something first." She leads us behind the altar into a narrow room. "You'll notice the crutches that line the walls. It's said the people who put them there have been cured by the sacred sand. If you look down there," she says, pointing to a small chamber at one end of the hall, "you'll see pilgrims kneeling at a shrine. When they finish praying, they'll reach down and scoop up some of the sand and rub it on their bodies, hoping for a miracle."

The hall where we stand smells of mildew and candle wax and something else, perhaps incense, perhaps the perfume worn by the heavily made-up woman ahead of me whose bracelets jingle as she enters the chamber. Not only crutches line these walls. I see dog tags and rosaries and photographs of children, and I pull back, feeling like an intruder. We watch the woman kneel in the dirt, complete her devotions, then rub sand on her shoulders. She uses a slow, circular motion to apply the sand to the bodice of her brightly colored dress, and then to her ample belly. Eyes closed, she moves her lips silently.

"Praying for a miracle," Tess observes.

"Do you believe in them?" Kevin asks her, his voice somber, respectfully low.

"Do you?" she counters in a whisper.

Overwhelmed, I fumble for a Kleenex in the pocket of my jeans and pretend to read some of the letters that pilgrims have fastened to the walls. The light is dim. I squint through tears and distinguish just scrawls. I can only guess: *Save me from this terrible affliction and I will promise you anything.*

When I look up, Kevin and Tess have already left. At first I wonder how she managed to support his weight, but then I remember how strong she's become. All that stretching and running. As I pass through the chamber I notice the kneeprints of the faithful and the depression in the sand pit where pilgrims have scratched up handfuls to rub on their skin. Who fills the pit? I wonder. A caretaker? God?

Outside, under a sun that startles with its brilliance, I find them, heads together, murmuring. She brushes something from his shirt. Sand? Does he believe in miracles? Should I? They seem unaware of my presence, yet I know that can't be so. After all, I am the connecting link, the cement that bonds them.

It's our last night in Santa Fe.

Tess has decided to cook fish on the outdoor grill, so she and I go shopping, leaving Kevin and Ermine to finish their afternoon naps. On the way back from the market she asks, "Have you thought about my offer? This would be the perfect place for you to heal. I can't see you staying on in your apartment, or moving in with your parents."

The salmon steaks we bought weigh only a couple of pounds, but suddenly they feel much heavier on my knees. "How can you expect me to give you an answer *now?*" I say. "He's still alive, for Christ's sake!" I think, *She doesn't have a clue about my life at this moment. Maybe she never did. All she ever cared about was her own situation.* "How can you be so insensitive?" I shout. "You don't give a shit about me. This is all about you, isn't it? Nothing's changed!"

Tess grips the wheel, slows down, pulls into someone's driveway. "Look who's calling who selfish!" she yells. A woman opens her front door and stares at us, two angry women screaming at each other, and for a minute I wonder if she's going to call the police. "We had plans after graduation. You backed out of my life without even so much as an apology. Jesus, Laura. I *adored* you. But then you were too fucking wrapped up in Kevin to notice!"

"So that's what this is about," I say. "With Kevin out of the way, I mean *really* out of the way, you're gonna make a move on me!"

She inhales sharply and turns away, shading her eyes. "Don't flatter yourself."

Tess and I sulk in the woman's driveway. Sweat trickles down our necks. The fish is beginning to stink in the oppressive mid-afternoon heat, and the smell is making me nauseous. I think about the time I saw salmon swimming upstream to spawn. What was it that Kevin said? *Against all odds.* We were on our honeymoon, camping in the Cascades. In Leavenworth, we got drunk at a sidewalk café and bought postcards. I sent one to Tess: *Wish you were here (not really).*

Talk about insensitive.

I reach over and touch the hand that's folded against her cheek. Her fingers are moist. "Tess. Please forgive me." Are there words that will ever make things right between us? I wonder.

She forces a laugh. "Oh, who gives a fuck?" she shouts, gunning the motor. We peel out, leaving the woman angrily shaking her fist at us for disturbing her peace.

At the airport in Albuquerque, Tess waits while we check our bags, then disappears. When she returns she's carrying a small paper sack, which she gives to Kevin. "When we were at the *santuario* I meant to get you one of these," she says. "It's a kind of religious good-luck charm. You're supposed to carry it with you at all times. To ward off evil spirits."

He forces a smile. "A little late for good luck, wouldn't you say?"

We stand in awkward silence. Finally I ask, "Do you think you'll be coming east for Christmas?"

She shrugs. "I doubt I'll have the money," she says, letting me off the hook.

"You could stay with us," Kevin offers affably. In the last few days he seems to have undergone a sea change. Before, he regarded her warily as one would a rival. Now he welcomes her to our house, *our* shrine.

"Thanks." She bends stiffly forward to embrace us both, opening her arms wide, planting kisses in the air, avoiding our eyes. "Safe trip, you two. Don't forget to write."

I had a little speech all ready but at the last minute I choke and can only brush her dry cheek with my lips. Then, in an unrehearsed move of defiance, I put my arms around Kevin as if to say, *He's in my keeping; this is where I belong,* but when I look up she's already slipped away. I imagine her running all the way to her car, arms pumping, sandals slapping the pavement, knowing, as I do, that we'll never see each other again.

When the plane taxis down the runway I feel perspiration bead on my palms, but before Kevin can ask me *Are you scared?* we're airborne. As the plane banks, passengers peer out the windows at the ground. Kevin, excited as always by the adventure of flying, grins at me and says, "Do you remember the first time we traveled together? It was our honeymoon. We vowed we'd take vacations every year, even if we had to borrow the money. Weren't we the reckless little devils?"

I turn away from him and pretend to look across the aisle and out the window on the other side. Of course there's nothing to see there, just clouds and blue sky and the edge of the wing that shines in the sunlight like the blade of a knife. Kevin swallows a pill and closes his eyes, and I know he's impatient for results. He also wants an answer. "Yes," I say finally. "We had nothing to lose."

DEPTH OF FIELD

"Remember," Garrett told Sarah as he guided her into the car, "you're going because you want to. Nobody's making you do this. Just remember that when the going gets rough."

"I know," she said, taking her camera bag from his outstretched hand and accepting his kiss. He worried that she and their daughter Itsy would end up fighting, as they so often did, and she shared his concern. And yet she was going anyway, driving for three hours on interstates, riding a ferry across Lake Champlain, then driving some more—all of this just so she could tell her friends she'd visited the love nest, the apartment Itsy shared with her lover, Wayne, in a dreary little upstate town.

Friends had told her they wouldn't do it. "Why put your stamp on something you don't approve of in the first place?" they asked.

"Oh, come on," Sarah countered. "Everybody lives together these days. Don't you read the birth notices in the paper? Babies have their mothers' last names." At least Itsy isn't pregnant yet, she thought. "Besides, I like Wayne," she insisted. This wasn't a lie. She did like him. He was good-looking and had a sense of humor, and the fact that he didn't seem to have any sense of direction in his life wasn't really her problem, anyway; it was his, and Itsy's.

"He drives trucks?" Garrett asked the first time Itsy told them about Wayne. "That's what he does for a living? What, is he working his way through college or something?"

"He didn't go to college, Dad. Not everybody does, you know," Itsy replied, bristling.

"Truck drivers make good money," Sarah remembered saying in Wayne's defense. "Especially the ones who go across the country." Now when she traveled, she could no longer see a rig without thinking of him and wondering whether he missed Itsy as much as she'd like him to.

When Sarah finally reached the ferry, it was raining, and there was a line of cars waiting—people anxious to get home for the weekend, she imagined. She could see the boat making its way slowly toward the landing, dragging seagulls in its wake. The last time she rode the ferry, Garrett was driving, and she didn't pay attention. Did people stay in their cars once on board, or did they get out? She couldn't remember. Years of traveling with Garrett had made her a lazy observer, but her new interest in photography was forcing her to take note of even the tiniest details. She'd found a non-credit course at the local community college and signed up on a whim, wanting to acquire some basic skills. Soon she learned to elicit praise from the instructor. "Good seeing, Mrs. Boyd!" he'd enthuse, his face lighting up with pleasure. He was incredibly young, just a couple of years older than Itsy, she guessed, but he seemed to know what he was doing. "Think of your camera as another pair of eyes," he used to tell the class. And she did. She had one of the new automatic SLRs, easy to use as is, but with the option of greater challenge if she switched to manual. She took her camera everywhere and used it as an excuse to surreptitiously explore her surroundings. By the end of the course she'd lost some of her innate shyness; even Garrett noticed a change. "Photography's good for you," he said. You need something now that Itsy's gone." Sarah resented his benediction, wanting her newfound passion to be private. Now that she had rediscovered the wet pebbles glistening in the driveway, the shriveled apples clinging to branches in October, the mist rising like gauze on frosty mornings, she felt obliged to capture those sights on film. But like a writer who is superstitious about revealing the plot of the next novel, she wouldn't discuss her feelings with Garrett.

She chided herself for momentarily forgetting what it was like to ride the ferry, as this was her fourth visit to Itsy in less than a year. "You've got to learn to let go," her friends admonished, but Sarah paid them no heed. Itsy was her one and only, and had rarely been away from home. "Once a mother, always a mother," she'd joke, thinking her friends callous for wanting her to cut the cord. She knew there'd come a time when she'd have to back off. What did they think she was, stupid?

Now keys were being turned in ignitions and cars were beginning to inch forward toward the dockhand in the yellow slicker who was signaling them to advance. Sarah remembered that the cars in the front row had blocks in front of their wheels to prevent slippage in the event of choppy waters, and she knew the minute those blocks were removed, the air would be thick with exhaust. The rain-splattered windshield reminded her of wrinkled cellophane, so she lined up a camera shot, flicking off the lens cap, letting her breath out slowly, counting to three before pressing the shutter-release button. She'd begun to shoot a roll of black and white and was anticipating good results. "You seem to understand what I'm saying," Tad, the instructor, told her once. His hand had brushed hers and she'd felt a shiver of delight before she reminded herself she was old enough to be his mother.

Five minutes after leaving the ferry—Itsy said it might take longer, depending on traffic—and surprised that Itsy's written directions were so clear, she was parking her car in front of the house (old brown clapboards in need of paint) and walking up the porch stairs to push a bell beneath a small hand-lettered sign that read ISABEL BOYD AND WAYNE LAMARTINE. Who had ever called her Isabel?

Sarah remembered giving her the toddler nickname of Itsabel because she was so tiny, and it stuck, shortened to Itsy. It was the only name they'd ever used, but now, apparently, there was a need to be more formal. And Wayne with his French-Canadian forebears. Such an elegant name, Lamartine. Too elegant for a doorbell that didn't work and a porch that needed to be painted and a front door with two cracked windowpanes.

Itsy opened the door and issued a warm welcome. "Mom!" she said, smiling, and Sarah melted in her embrace. *This is where I should be,* she thought. *To hell with what people think.* As they climbed to the second landing, Sarah caught her heel on a piece of metal that had come loose, part of the aluminum strip that anchored a well-worn stair tread. "Well? What do you think? Isn't it terrific? I mean, for five hundred fifty dollars a month. And we have our own backyard!" Itsy paused, waiting for Sarah's approval, but when it didn't come, she continued. "Okay, I know it needs to be painted. The landlord says he'll do it next spring, outside and in."

They entered the apartment through the living room, where Sarah recognized the couch she and Itsy had selected the year before. The rest of the furniture—a tall cabinet containing a television set, stereo components and a shelf that held a football and some trophies—belonged to Wayne. There were no books. Garrett would be horrified, Sarah thought. "I'll put you in here, in our little guest room," Itsy said as they stepped into a cubicle barely big enough to hold a cot and the small maple bureau she'd grown up with. Worn stuffed animals, old friends from Itsy's childhood, lined a shelf above the bed, and next to that hung a bulletin board with snapshots from last Christmas: Itsy with her dog, Wayne in front of the tree looking bored, Sarah in the kitchen with her head cut off (Itsy had taken that one), Garrett proudly using his new snowblower on the driveway. It pleased Sarah to see that Itsy had furnished this room by herself and that she had tenderly created a little island of childhood keepsakes, even though she was now Isabel and living with a man.

"Come see the rest of the apartment. Wayne won't be home till late tonight, so we have the place to ourselves. Did you want to go out to dinner? There's a Mexican restaurant not far from here. Or, if you'd rather, we can do take-out Chinese." As Sarah followed Itsy into the bedroom she shared with Wayne, she noticed, with distaste, the fake fur bedspread. There was also a second, smaller television set; a couple of framed team photos on the wall; a rowing machine; and a set of weights. No sign of Itsy here, Sarah thought, although she knew better; her daughter's invisible aura would be everywhere.

Beyond the bedroom was the bathroom, with two robes hung on the back of the door. At first Sarah found it amusing that Itsy's short pink terry wrap dangled, as always, by its sleeve instead of from the loop on the inside of the neck. But when she saw Wayne's kimono thrown over it, the robes seemed to characterize the whole living arrangement, and Sarah sensed that the apartment, formerly his, now still belonged only to him.

When she realized she'd have to pass through their bedroom to get to the bathroom at night, she said, "I should have stayed in a motel."

"I wanted you to be here, with me. With us."

"I feel like an intruder."

Itsy rolled her eyes. "Get over it, Mom. *We* don't feel funny, so why should you?"

"Are you *sure?*"

"Of course I'm sure." They moved into the kitchen. "Hey. Chill out. Have a beer. Sorry we're fresh out of French wine, which I know you'd prefer."

"Beer would be fine," Sarah said, accepting a bottle of Bud Light and a New England Patriots mug.

"Want me to pour?"

"Absolutely not. Just because I don't drink the stuff doesn't mean I don't know how it's done," she said, tipping the bottle and the mug to minimize the head, as she'd seen Garrett do. "I don't suppose you have a coaster."

Itsy laughed. "Are you kidding?" She handed Sarah a napkin that advertised Louie's Sports Bar. "You're lucky I gave you a mug."

"What about all those kitchen supplies I gave you for your other apartment?"

"You mean the things from Gram's house? I have most of it around here somewhere. See, this is Wayne's place, Mom, and he already has all his stuff. Nothing matches, of course, but that doesn't bother me." She gave her mother a determined look. *So butt out!*

Sarah could feel her hackles rising. "My mother's Franciscan pottery. There was service for eight. What happened to *that?*" She struggled to keep her voice calm and even.

"Well, okay. You want the truth? I gave it away. Wayne doesn't like eating off flowered plates."

Sarah was stunned; she'd given her mother those dishes on a significant occasion—a major milestone, like a fiftieth birthday or a fortieth anniversary, and to have them tossed aside like garbage was more than she could bear. For a moment she regretted making the trip. Then she remembered Garrett's words: *Nobody's making you do this.* She hadn't unpacked her bag. It would be so easy to leave, but then she'd feel the shame of her own anger all the way home. Better to stay and be forgiving. She wrapped the sweating mug in a napkin, breathed deeply, and exhaled slowly while Itsy waited, eyes lowered, for a scolding. Then Sarah surprised them both by saying, "Well, honey, you have a really nice place here."

During dinner at Rosa's Cantina, Sarah watched her daughter push food around her plate. "Something's bothering you," she said finally. "Come on. Out with it."

"It's nothing, really," Itsy took a pack of cigarettes from her purse and lit one. She took only a couple of puffs, then ground it out in a ceramic ashtray that was shaped like a sombrero. "Okay, but I don't want you blaming Wayne." She searched her mother's eyes as if to extract a promise.

Here it comes, Sarah thought. *How can I not be judgmental?* "I know it takes two," she said evasively. "So what happened?"

Itsy stifled a sob. "We had a fight and I haven't seen him in a couple of days."

Sarah turned back the clock and saw a small child in a sandbox after a fight with a friend; then, as now, Itsy wiped away tears with the back of her hand. "Oh, baby, I'm sorry," Sarah said, reaching across to touch her daughter's face.

"I'm not a baby anymore, Mom."

"I know." Sarah wanted to take Itsy by the shoulders and shake some sense into her. *It's hard to stand back and watch you ruin your life like this.* So much promise, so little to show for it, Garrett might say.

"I think Wayne feels I shouldn't have moved in with him. But I did, and now I don't know what to do!"

I can tell you what to do: Move out. The words were there, waiting to be pushed from Sarah's lips, but she kept her silence. Garrett would be proud.

"I know you think I should move out, but it's not that simple. If I do that, it's over between us. I can't let that happen." Itsy blotted her cheek with the sleeve of her sweater and gulped her margarita.

Sarah stopped herself from using the napkin to brush the salt off Itsy's lips, realizing that such an action would be interpreted as a travesty, a reminder to Itsy that her mother still saw her as a child who needed adult supervision, instead of a full-grown woman who was responsible for her own life and the mess she sometimes made of it.

"I love him," Itsy continued. "I know it's hard for you to understand, because he's not like anybody I grew up with, not somebody you or Daddy would have chosen for me. But I *do* love him."

The waitress stopped by to see if everything was all right. "Refills?" she asked, pointing to the near-empty glasses.

Sarah nodded, then watched Itsy light another cigarette. "I didn't know you were smoking again. What happened to last year's good health resolution?"

Itsy shrugged. "Wayne smokes, and it seems easier to join him."

"Ah." She waited, wondering if she ought to pose the next question that logically presented itself in her mind. *What the hell.* "You don't smoke pot, though. Right?"

"Mom." Itsy smiled tolerantly. "Everybody smokes pot."

Back at the apartment, they watched television and, during commercial breaks, discussed Itsy's job as a teacher's aide. Sarah wished she would go back to college and get her degree so she could really teach, but Itsy already knew her mother's feelings on the subject, so there was no point in having a discussion.

When the program ended, Itsy asked, "Do you mind if I turn in, Mom? I'm really sleepy all of a sudden. Must be the margaritas."

"Hey, I'm tired, too," Sarah responded, forcing a laugh. "You know me. A cheap drunk." She was secretly relieved to be off the hook as far as Itsy's professional plans were concerned, knowing she'd have expressed an opinion eventually. Itsy's mood had lightened somewhat since dinner, but Sarah could sense her daughter's deep-seated unhappiness and wished there was something she could do to help. *You wouldn't want to bunk with your old ma, now, would you? It'd be like old times, when you used to climb into bed with us to escape those bad dreams.* "Look, baby. You said you don't know *when* he's coming back, but you know he *is* coming back, right?"

Sarah pretended to fall asleep, but it was impossible to ignore her daughter's pain as long as Itsy tossed restlessly in the next room and occasionally cried. Without a watch (hers was at home, probably on the kitchen windowsill where she'd put it before doing the breakfast dishes), Sarah couldn't tell the exact time, but at some hour, perhaps halfway through the night, Wayne returned.

The walls were so thin that Sarah could hear almost everything. "You never think of what I need. You always think about yourself. Who was it this time?" Itsy asked. They were in the kitchen. Sarah strained to hear Wayne's response, but he dropped his voice until it was just above a whisper. "Only friends"? Was that what he said? Then Itsy began to cry. It was almost more than Sarah could bear. When they moved out of the kitchen and into the bedroom and closed the door behind them, she put her face in her pillow and wept.

Although circumstances prevented her from doing otherwise, she felt embarrassed to be eavesdropping. Her friends were right. It was wrong to interfere. While she had no way of knowing how bad the timing would be, she should have stayed home. Wayne certainly didn't want her around, and Itsy had asked her to come only out of a sense of, what, duty? Or had she wanted her mother to see, first-hand, the trouble she was in?

In an effort to clear her head, she got out of bed and opened the small window that overlooked a brightly lit street. Despite the late hour, there were people passing by, on foot and in cars. She was reminded of another street and another time, and of the fact that she and Garrett had come from different backgrounds. They'd also had parents who were eager to make things right. Now she realized there were some things that couldn't be made right. "Anybody can take a picture that's been taken a thousand times before. The trick is to take a picture that nobody's ever taken," her photography instructor declared. "Even if it's off-kilter, or the subject seems odd. There's nothing fascinating about perfection."

When Sarah tiptoed into the bathroom the next morning, she saw Itsy and Wayne asleep in each other's arms.

She left a note on the kitchen table: "Forgive me for sneaking off so early. Had a nice visit. Love, Mom."

Before she got into her car, she looked back at the house, thinking that if Itsy had heard her leave, she might have come to say goodbye. She would have welcomed a chance to tell her daughter she understood. In the absence of such a sentimental parting, though, she felt the need to pause for a moment, to fix in her mind the image of the house where Itsy had chosen to live with Wayne. At first, all she saw was the unremarkable front door with its scarred wood panels and cracked panes, but then she took out her camera and seized what some great photographer has called *the decisive moment*. She did this not because Garrett would want to see where the children lived, but because she needed to capture that perfectly unperfect, ordinary door on film. There was no other reason at all.

ORDINARY PERILS

All week Lillian has imagined herself saying, "I've been thinking we've come to a crossroad in our lives," a line suggested by her recently divorced, kooky friend, Fran, but as she and David approach their weekend destination, she decides it's too dramatic, too Fran, and opts instead for "I know this will be hurtful, but I've given it a lot of thought," which is true—she *has* given the matter a lot of thought. As they begin the familiar ascent up the access road north of Rutland that leads to the inn, Lillian leans forward, opens the glove compartment, and takes out a package of sugar-free gum. She'd prefer a cigarette, but since she's given them up, she does the next best thing—shoves a frozen stick in her mouth and holds the cinnamon-scented package under his nose. "Want some?" she asks.

He shakes his head, concentrating on the road, which narrows, then twists and turns as they climb higher. "Is anything wrong?" he asked the night before. When she didn't answer, he said, "Okay. Be evasive. But don't expect me to be a mind reader. These days, I never know what's up with you." This makes her think it won't be hard to tell him.

"He'd be a fool to think you've been happy," Fran said, "because you two haven't been on the same wavelength for months. Am I right?" Lillian agreed that everything had changed the day

David lost his vision temporarily in one eye and had to be rushed to the emergency room of the hospital where he had been delivering babies for twenty-five years. While he was being diagnosed with a blocked carotid artery, he was in the care of friendly colleagues, which must have seemed odd, since David was used to treating himself. They recommended surgery, which he refused. After his discharge from the hospital, he took a disability leave—"Just to get my sea legs"—during which Lillian felt she was living a bipolar nightmare. One minute he was his old confident self, the next, a helpless child needing reassurance every step of the way. She worried that he'd never return to work, yet wondered what would happen if he did. Suppose he was as moody in the delivery room as he was at home. What then? "The truth is, Lillian, he could have a stroke anytime." The cardiologist's dire warning, issued in the chilly atmosphere of the coronary-care unit, had sobered them both.

In subsequent months, he seemed overwhelmed by a fear of dying. She'd always counted on him to be lighthearted when circumstances ran against them; instead, he became a sad and apprehensive stranger, a hapless victim of fate. What could she do but try to protect him from the ordinary perils of life? She saw that he took his beta-blockers every morning, and that he checked his blood pressure every night. With her help, he seemed to have everything under control, yet she sensed he felt compelled to test himself at every turn. In bed, for instance. An unfortunate side effect of his medication was that it tended to make him impotent. She tried to be understanding. "Everybody has these problems in middle age," she'd say, rubbing his back, trying to minimize his embarrassment by being affectionate. She'd assure him it was no big deal, even as she was admitting to herself the distance between them was greatest when they lay beside each other in bed.

When he announced, after six weeks, that he was going back to his practice, she felt an overwhelming sense of relief. At Fran's urging, she'd already started thinking about leaving him, but hadn't dared raise the subject while he was still recuperating. She'd admitted to Fran that sex had become just another lackluster routine, like going to the dry cleaner. "Face it, honey," Fran said. "There were problems before his illness."

In subsequent months, a new-age therapist convinced Lillian she needed to get her own life in order before she decided to end her marriage (easier said than done,) and a pastoral counselor suggested a couples retreat might improve their communication (David refused to go). When the Prozac her doctor prescribed gave her headaches and diarrhea, Lillian let Fran drag her to the Y for step aerobics. "There's nothing like exercise to cure the blues," Fran said, certain Lillian would fit right in with the women in the class, but Lillian quit after only three sessions, saying the complicated routines made her feel like a klutz. "You're not doing anything to help yourself," Fran scolded. By this time, she was beginning to annoy Lillian with her know-it-all attitude. "Women our age have a choice—we can continue to live boring lives or we can make our own excitement," Fran said. Obviously, she had learned to live by this dictum. She'd left her husband, a sweet, stable otolaryngologist, for an impoverished scatterbrain fifteen years her junior who ended up dumping her, and now she'd found herself an older female companion, a lesbian who'd only recently launched a business of importing Scottish shortbread and selling it to tony shops in upscale malls. None of this seemed exciting to Lillian.

Although Fran was encouraging Lillian to end her marriage, she also warned her of the consequences. "You've gotta be prepared," she cautioned. "The medical community will shun you. And David won't waste any time in remarrying. With all those sexy young professionals eager to hook up with a successful older guy? I give him six months, tops."

Lillian already envied the young female practitioners at David's clinic, especially the married ones whose stay-at-home husbands drove youngsters in car pools while running consulting businesses from their basements. What she would have given for a meaningful career instead of her thankless role as David's appendage. "So what if he remarries right away? I intend to savor my freedom!" she declared in a flash of Fran-inspired bravado as her friend poured Beaujolais from a carafe and they clinked glasses, toasting independence.

After lunch that day, Lillian let Fran lead her down a nearby street to a little shop called Private Moments, where sex toys and videos were sold. She'd heard about the place from one of David's colleagues, at a cocktail party when he joked about the kinky merchandise. "I don't think I want to do this," she said as Fran marched her inside, where a husky, pleasant-faced woman greeted them.

"Hey, Fran. Where've you been? Daphne was here last week. She looks *great.* Must be love, huh?" Daphne was Fran's new partner. Lillian waited for her friend to respond, but Fran had already drifted to the back of the store, to the room where videos were displayed. "Looking for something in particular?" the proprietor asked Lillian. "First time here? Let me show you around. Don't worry," she said, when she sensed Lillian's reluctance to explore. "There's no obligation to buy. Let's start with the mini-vibrators, the purse models, battery operated, very discreet . . ."

For the next half hour, Lillian's eyes were opened to a new world of sexual exploration—penises made of simulated skin that vibrated, promising the ultimate experience in pleasure and stimulation, and an array of scary utensils, for inserter and insertee, as well as a line of naturally contoured products with names like Femme and Magnifique, which struck her as vaguely appealing, and nipple clamps, which made her wince. When she made her selection, an innocent-looking four-inch-long pocket vibrator, Fran met her at the register carrying a stack of rental videos.

In the car, Lillian glanced at the titles: *Hot Bods in Action, Beach Baby Bingo, Naughty Nurses, Wild Women.* "Are they any good?" she asked Fran. "I mean artistically."

Fran laughed. "Daphne loves them. Why don't you come over and see for yourself?"

Lillian glanced at her watch. "Thanks, but no. I've got to . . ."

"Get home in time to make him dinner. Oh, yeah, baby. I know the drill. I'll drop you off then, but keep us in mind one night when the boss is busy."

Later that afternoon, Lillian turned on her television set, perused the pay-per-view menu, and began to experience the endless tangle of bad actors heaving and panting and thrusting as they simulated sex. All those silicone implants and impeccably groomed pubes! She longed for a plot; even the male actors looked bored. What she really wanted was some sign of tenderness, that appealing aspect of passion she'd come to miss in the months since David's diagnosis.

As for the pocket vibrator, it was relegated to the back of her lingerie drawer, where it rested, unopened, until she finally decided to throw it away.

Lillian is thinking about her recent foray into soft porn as David pulls into the parking lot at the inn. "Why don't you go ahead and register?" he suggests. "I'll bring in the bags."

"Wait. I'll get someone to help you," she says, lifting the garment bag out of the backseat and imagining the look he's giving her behind his aviator glasses. "He's so defensive," she'd told the cardiologist. "It's driving me crazy." In response, the doctor had only shrugged. He'd given her a book, *After Illness, Then What?* which she skimmed, found lacking, and donated to the library's rummage sale. Racy movies were more amusing, especially the titles, which kept coming to mind at the least opportune moments, like now, as she unloads their trunk. *Vixens on Vacation.* Had she really seen that one, or did she make it up?

Upstairs, in the familiar confines of the room they'd stayed in so often they'd come to call it their own, she stands at the window and watches the guests skin snow off their skis. She knows that soon the new, younger guests will gather around a crackling fire to sip cocoa or mulled cider from earthenware mugs and pass their drowsy babies back and forth like sacks of sand. At times like these, Lillian feels the old sadness deeply. She and David had wanted so much to have children. Maybe that was the beginning of her sense of isolation, when she realized there would be no children, there'd just be the two of them, he working long hours at the clinic, she waiting for him at home. Maybe she should have made her move then, she thinks.

When David appears with the luggage, she reaches for a suitcase, but he brushes past her into the room and dumps the whole lot on the floor in front of the closet. "I'm fine, I'm fine," he insists. "I took the stairs two at a time just to see if I could. That's why I'm bushed." He hesitates before adding defensively, "*Anybody* would be." He sits down in an armchair and props up his feet on the end of the bed. "Just give me a minute, okay?" With his thinning hair and flushed face, he appears much older to her. She can see he's sweating. Damn! This is her fault. If she hadn't been so anxious to get up to their room, she could have waited for him in the entryway. She could have insisted that he get help. These days he seems to need her protection at every turn, yet every attempt provokes the same response: *I'm fine, I'm not an invalid, why do you keep treating me like one?*

Years ago, David had been a reckless winter athlete, seeking out every difficult trail on the mountain, while she, hating the cold and fearing injury, sat out part of each afternoon in the base lodge. In those years, a morning on the slopes was enough for her, but he'd stay out until the lifts closed, showing up just as she was about to call the ski patrol. His then bearded face crusty with ice and ruddy from the wind, he'd boast, "I got all the way down the north face!"

Now that they are firmly middle-aged and have shifted from alpine to nordic, they ski together, more or less. Even so, if he wants to stay out longer, she can always retreat to their comfortable room to read or nap. The room is the best the inn has to offer—tastefully furnished with chintz-covered chairs, an early-American-style quilt, and Audubon prints on the wall—with a spectacular view of the reservoir. The season before, she'd been greeted by the sight of flame red maples; now she looks down on a sloping expanse of white fringed with gray sticks, bare trees that line the sledding hill behind the main lodge where small children are being arranged on toboggans, their snowsuits splashing color on the landscape. At noon, clouds are moving in, fulfilling a forecast of snow, but for the moment the hill is bathed in bright sunshine. As she hears peals of laughter, Lillian thinks, If we'd had children, we'd be bringing our grandchildren here now. All that cooing over other people's babies has worn her thin, turned her bitter. She pictures herself, in her new life, living in an adults-only community, in a resort area somewhere warm, far away from the squawking of newborns. There she'll live life the way she's always wanted, with no more social role-playing, and no one to pity the obstetrician's barren wife. *Luscious Ladies Get It On.*

If there have been times when she's felt she'd be better off staying married, she quickly remembers Fran's observations about some of the clinic retirees: "Those formerly hardworking, hunky, handsome guys who've been cast adrift like shipwrecked sailors, those plump-gutted sloths who spend their days lounging around the house waiting for the cocktail hour, wanting their wives to do everything with them? That wouldn't be for you, honey." Fran was right. David doesn't have any hobbies, doesn't play golf. A new start is what she needs, although she can't imagine dating at her age, and when she considers the possibility of taking a younger lover, she cringes at the thought of becoming a sixties-movie joke, a predatory older female. Cowed by the thought of picking up someone in a singles bar, she recalls Fran's experiences and concedes that although it might be possible for her to do this, it's highly unlikely she would. And Lillian admits she's never been sexually attracted to other women, so she can forget the lesbian scene. "You've got to make your move soon, Lil. Let him take you skiing one more time, then lower the boom."

Two hours later, she and David are standing in front of the ski school hut, brushing snow off their skis. "Let's just do the loop once," he says. "That way we'll be all set for tomorrow. Once around'll give us the lay of the land." Lillian is reluctant because it's already three o'clock and snowing so heavily she can hardly see. When she bends over to check her bindings, her goggles fog up. It's so cold her bare fingers, which she's exposed to zip her jacket, are already numb. The plus is that they'll probably have the trails all to themselves; who'd want to be outdoors in weather like this? She's always a little nervous the first time out; this way, nobody will see her falter. "All set?" he asks.

"Wait." She can feel the wet snow sneaking into the tiny space between her collar and the back of her neck, so she pulls the neck warmer out of her pocket and slips it over her head. "Now I'm ready."

It always takes awhile to hit her stride. Then, if the tracks are well groomed and she's feeling energetic, they'll ski in sync, two figures gliding on the wide, flat part of the trail, graceful and serene, and, to the casual observer, completely in concert with each other.

They follow the markers and ascend an intermediate slope slowly, he hopping ahead, herringboning, and she climbing sideways, digging in the edge of her uphill ski so that she won't slip. Halfway up, he stops. She sees that he's breathing heavily. "You okay?" He nods, unable to speak. "Wait a minute. Take it slow. We can turn back anytime, you know." He shakes his head, pauses for another couple of seconds, then resumes the climb. There's a reward ahead: a long, slow descent through some woods and, at the bottom of the trail, a warming hut. She does a kick turn and faces the other direction. This way she can see across the meadow where the outline of the inn, shrouded in falling snow, is barely visible. As she watches, the outside lights flick on, a reminder of twilight.

At the top of the hill, while Lillian pauses to wipe her goggles and blow her nose, David surges ahead. Around her, the cold, crisp air is charged with sounds—the zip of fish scales on hard-packed snow, the cawing of crows, the rasp of her own breath. Once she's beneath the protective canopy of trees, branches creak overhead. She can feel her heart thudding from the effort of poling and striding. Why can't he wait? She knows the answer—he has to prove to himself he can ski the loop in forty-five minutes, his record.

Now she skis out of the woods and sees, ahead and slightly to the right, the warming hut, where smoke is curling from the chimney. She remembers that sometimes the trail groomers light a fire, but that they rely on the skiers to keep it going by adding a log or two when they stop in to warm up. She skis down to the hut and releases her bindings, intending to enter the hut, recalling words David once uttered in jest, "Wouldn't this be the perfect place for a quickie?" She notices two pairs of skis propped against the side of the hut and imagines a young couple, he straddling the bench and she with her legs wrapped around his waist. When she leans back, the woman's breasts will be bare, her long blond hair will brush the floor. *Nordic Nannies at Play*. She stands there quietly for a few minutes in the stillness of falling snow, waiting to hear the woman cry out. She feels her own skin burn, although beneath the layers of clothing she's growing damp and chilled. As she turns away, she's surprised by the power of her eroticism. These days, everything seems to lie just below the surface, ready to burst forth at the slightest provocation.

When she reaches the inn, he's waiting, his face flushed by cold and exertion. "What took you so long? I was beginning to worry. It's pretty awful out there."

"Sorry." As Lillian stands in the foyer and unzips her jacket, she imagines she can see the girl with the long blond hair gliding gracefully across the field, her lover by her side, their silhouettes barely visible in the dusk. For a moment she considers telling David about her fantasy, but adds instead, "I didn't mean to worry you."

"I did the loop in fifty minutes. Not bad, huh? Hey. You with me?" He hangs their jackets on some hooks and leans their skis against the wall where melting clumps of snow have pooled. "Whaddya say we hit the bar, for old times' sake? You used to say *après-ski* was your favorite part of the day. Remember?"

They'd finish the day with a sauna, then shower. Later, they'd sip martinis by the fire and enjoy a bottle of wine with dinner. In those days, their lovemaking was vigorous and noisy. There was a loose headboard that used to clatter when she climaxed—they joked about it for months, hoping the people in the next room hadn't heard.

That night, they leave the curtains open, but soon it becomes evident that not even the magic of a winter moon can make things right. When he tries to compensate, she senses in his touch, as she has so many times before, a fierce determination that dampens her ardor. She pushes him away, thinking how sad all this is, wanting to reassure him, yet knowing from experience it's better to say nothing.

He apologizes. "I can't seem to do anything right. Sometimes I wonder if anything will ever be the same between us."

Here's the opening she's been waiting for, but no, she can't tell him in such an intimate setting, can't risk having him cry because then she, too, will cry, and they will talk things out and he will convince her not to leave him. "I'll give you a back rub," she says instead. That seems safe, something you do to soothe a child. There is no heavy emotional investment in a back rub.

Suddenly she recalls their conversation that evening in the dining room. "They have *mousse au chocolat,*" David said, brandishing the dessert menu, his expression gleefully, adorably childish. "You're not going to give me an argument, are you?" She tries to imagine how it must feel to plead for pudding. In the old days, he'd never have let her push him around. Lillian realizes how much she's been yearning for a glimpse of someone she knew years ago, someone who just skied down the north face of a mountain and scared her half to death by not showing up at the lodge in time. It's this loss she's been mourning, this loss that has rendered her incapable of feeling passion without some kind of kinky stimulus like a stupid sex video. As the image of the couple in the ski hut returns, she stops rubbing his back. "David," she whispers, "are you awake?"

At breakfast he says, "I heard someone say they closed our favorite trail, the one that snakes through the meadow. Ice, I guess."

"Well, you'll have to ski the upper trails, then."

"You're not coming?"

"No, I . . ." Here she longs for a pulled muscle, something that will legitimize her refusal. Hell, why not just say it? "Actually, I'd rather read." He shrugs, obviously disappointed. "I *really* don't feel like skiing. It has nothing to do with . . . anything else," she adds lamely, but she can see from the bruised look in his eyes it's no use.

They finish eating in silence. She watches him fold his napkin neatly in thirds and place it carefully on the table. "Well, then. I guess I'll see you later," he says finally. When he guides her out of the dining room, she allows herself to be led, feeling the insistent pressure of his fingers against her elbow. Last night he touched her with dry, chapped fingers. In winter, his hands crack and bleed, part of the hazards of being a physician and having to wash a hundred times a day, even though gloves are worn when he reaches into women's vaginas. "Doesn't that ever bother you?" Fran asked once.

All morning the snow falls steadily, hampering visibility, making her glad she decided to stay in. By noon he will have completed the circuit of trails that begin just above the lodge and end on the other side of the warming hut; from their shared experiences, she knows the drill. At lunchtime she waits for him at the dining room entrance, but when he doesn't appear, she takes a sandwich and coffee upstairs.

Later, she tries to read the book she's brought, the biography of a lesser poet whose dismal life depresses her. Unable to concentrate on the arid prose, she moves from the easy chair to the writing desk, where she takes out a piece of inn stationery and begins a letter to an older cousin she hasn't seen in a decade. Lillian has heard, through family gossip channels, that the cousin's husband recently died of cancer. "Dear Beatrice," she begins, then hesitates, wondering if it's in bad taste to write a letter of condolence on hotel stationery. She crumples the sheet of paper and tosses it into the basket, kicks off her shoes, and crawls under the quilt. Sleep is better than a soap opera, the home shopping network, or Oprah—shows she could watch on the television set in the lounge were she not, suddenly, so very sleepy.

When she wakes, it's dark outside, and David hasn't returned. Annoyed, she thinks it's just like him to push his limits. With all his talk of the old days inflating his bravado, she guesses he'll stay out until they sweep the trails for stragglers. Then where? To the bar? It doesn't open till five. Besides, he'd want to shower first. She slips on a pair of clogs, brushes her hair, and applies lip gloss, preparing to go down to the lobby to make some inquiries.

"Have you seen my husband?" Lillian asks the desk clerk, a stuffy Ivy League clone in his blue blazer and chinos.

"Not since this morning, ma'am."

If he'd stop scribbling and look up, she thinks, it would help. "Well, would you mind calling the ski patrol?" She can see her concern mirrored in the face of another employee who's standing in the background. Why did they hire such a cold fish to work at the reception desk? What happened to Warm and Helpful, the kid who used to make us feel at home? Struggling to remain calm, she wonders if David forgot to take his medicine. Would one missed dose bring on a stroke? She imagines him lying paralyzed in the snow. But suppose it's only a mild stroke? Chances are, he'd recover. With equal dread, she recalls Fran's harsh warning: "You don't want to end up a cranky caregiver, waiting for David to die." And what if he shows up intact, apologizing for having lost track of time, triumphant, laying the spoils of conquest at her feet?

At six, she's still sitting in the lobby, nursing a Scotch and soda. The bartender has already been by twice to ask if she'd like a refill, but she's said no, because drinking on an empty stomach makes her tipsy. In the dining room, the young couples have finished their appetizers, and their babies, tucked in padded carriers, will be getting ready to scream again. The older crowd, people she recognizes from the previous night, are sitting around the fireplace making lively conversation, waiting for the second seating.

"Excuse me." Someone taps her on the shoulder, and in her tightly coiled state, she jumps up to face the maintenance boy, the new-age hippie in long hair and overalls who checked the leaky faucet in their bathroom. Dressed for the outdoors in warm-ups and a parka, he seems even younger and more vulnerable than your ordinary hard-nosed ski bum juggling jobs to pay for room and board. "Uh, they wanted me to tell you they've found your husband."

"Thank God." Relief claims her, floods her senses, surprising her with its intensity. Her eyes fill with tears. "Is he—"

"They're making him wait a bit at the ski hut, just to make sure he's okay. I guess he lost his way, got off on the wrong trail." She realizes the kid is trembling, probably jittery from having to deliver such an important piece of news in front of a growing audience of strangers, who reach out to touch her in empathy. They can only imagine what she's been going through. Desperate for a cigarette, she scans the crowd for a source, then glimpses the NO SMOKING sign displayed over the bar. *Shit.*

She leans against the boy, taking refuge in his jacket, which smells of wood smoke, overwhelmed by emotions the kid can't possibly understand. Lillian knows he's embarrassed; she can tell by the way he initially resists the urge to comfort her. In a fleeting moment of comic relief, she thinks that Fran, in her pre-shortbread mode, would have known what to do with this window of opportunity. *Snow Bunnies in Heat.* "Hey, now, it's not like it's the end of the world," he consoles her, offering a crush of tissues from his back pocket. Lillian senses a perfunctory quality in this gesture, as if he's impatient to get on with the rest of his evening. And why not? She doesn't want to be a nuisance, and vows to pull herself together. When she returns the stares of those curious bystanders, she imagines they want to know what she's going to do next.

SAVING A LIFE

"You come upon a person with a deathlike appearance," the CPR instructor says. "Give me the sequence of events."

My partner and I look at each other, fishing for hints. Between us, Resusci-Annie lies armless and legless on her back, her lips stretched in rigor-mortis readiness to receive our lips, but first one of us has to slap her face, shake her shoulders, and ask, "Are you all right?"

My partner, a young girl who wants to be a lifeguard this summer, says, "Are you all right?" to me.

"Say it to Annie," the instructor prompts. "She's the one who's in trouble."

My partner repeats the question, waits for a second, then shouts "Help!" in a small voice that hardly conveys panic. It's okay, I think. This is just for practice. But then I remember it's our testing day. "Look, listen, and feel," I whisper.

"Oh, yeah." My partner bends down and caresses Annie's face with long blond hair that is poker-straight and slightly greasy. Lucy—that's my partner's name—uses a lot of makeup to cover her acne. I know from experience that the makeup will flake off on Annie's chin. When I wipe with the alcohol pads, I'll be sure to include that chin.

"Four quick breaths," I whisper.

At first Lucy forgets to pinch Annie's nose and doesn't get a seal. We both look at Annie's chest. Nothing happens. The instructor is off in another corner of the room checking some other people who have gotten all the way up to their two-person rescue routine. Lucy remembers to pinch, and Annie's chest heaves up and down. Lucy smiles at me when she has given her four quick breaths. "All *right!*" she says, and proceeds to the next stage, the giving of one breath every five seconds for a minute, after which she will check for a pulse.

Resusci-Annie doesn't care. She does this four, maybe five times a day. I think she looks like Vanessa Redgrave. On the wall is posted a large sign that reads RESPECT YOUR ANNIES! REMEMBER TO CLEAN AND STORE THEM PROPERLY!

"No pulse," Lucy says. Her voice is now edged with just the proper tinge of panic. "What do I do now? Never mind, I know." But before I can stop her she is pressing on Annie's abdomen and the instructor is looking down and shaking her head from side to side.

"The xiphoid. Find it."

"Oh, yeah," Lucy says. Beads of sweat are beginning to appear on her upper lip. Soon she starts pressing on the right spot and I begin to relax. Soon it will be my cue to say, "I know CPR; can I help?"

While I am taking my CPR test Graham, my ex, is having tea with my mother. Every once in a while, maybe two, three times a month, he calls her. He never calls me. But I know he'd like to. I also know he's afraid to talk to me. He can talk to my mother and, during the course of their conversation, he can ask her little things about me. "What's she doing these days? Who's she seeing? Has she gotten anything published? Did she ever do anything about . . ." He goes on and on. How do I know? My mother tells me.

He's still crazy about you," she says, giving me that mischievous little smile. "He'd take you back in a minute. I know. I can tell from the way he keeps asking about you."

"Tough titty," I say. Usually I'm doing something for my mother when we have these conversations, like shampooing her hair or polishing her nails. Mother's an invalid, confined to a wheelchair but still self-sufficient in most respects. But like many invalids, she enjoys being pampered. Graham used to wait on her all the time. Since our breakup she's become more self-reliant, but I know she misses all that extra attention. "One more rinse," I say as I pour water over her hair, shielding her eyes with my other hand. I'm using the shampoo tray that Graham gave her last Christmas. It was a thoughtful gift, so practical and so Graham. "It gets me annoyed when he pumps you for information about me," I say. "He should have the guts to come right out and ask me."

"You're getting soap in my eyes!"

"This is rinse water, Mother."

"Well, something stings."

I hate having to do this. I wish we could get a beautician to come to the apartment. Last week Mother asked me to pluck her eyebrows. I don't even bother to pluck my own! I said I couldn't. "You'll have to ask Myrtle the next time I take you to have your hair cut," I said.

"Mabel. Her name is Mabel."

"Now sit up and I'll towel-dry you," I say, not really caring if it's Myrtle or Mabel.

Mother slides back in her chair and holds her dripping hair with her hands. I pat gently at first, then rub vigorously. "Tell me if I'm hurting you." I suddenly realize I'm gritting my teeth. It's Graham who's really getting to me, but what should I expect from him? After all, I was the one who wanted to end our marriage.

"If you dry it too much, you're not going to be able to set it in rollers," Mother warns. I comb her wet hair, divide it into sections the way I've seen Mabel do it, and start to roll. Her scalp is pink from all the rubbing. I say I hate doing this, but when she's all combed out I feel very virtuous. "What would I do without you?" she purrs. She used to say that to Graham and, before Graham, to my father. "Wouldn't you like to go to Florida this winter? Unless, of course, you pass your real estate exam and get a job. You did say you were going to take the exam this fall."

"Did I? I don't remember."

"I even told Graham."

"Oh, well, then I'll certainly have to take the exam!"

Mother reaches up and touches my hands. "There's no need for that kind of reaction," she says. "Besides, if you don't take the exam, you'll be free to come south with me.

I pull my hands away. Another impasse: I'm damned if I do and damned if I don't.

"About Florida," my mother says. "If you don't want to go, we don't have to."

"I'll have to think about it. I may want to take that poetry seminar at the Y." Of course I know what kind of response this will elicit. Mother and Graham think that poetry is a waste of time—for me, at least. They think I should stick to writing newspaper features.

"I loved that piece she did on eggplant for the *Globe,*" Mother told her friends. "She could write a cookbook if she put her mind to it. There's a lot of money in cookbooks."

We are up to the part where we have to change positions. "Switch one thousand, two one thousand, three one thousand, four one thousand, breathe." There's no time to wipe Annie's mouth, so I just give her all I've got and check for a pulse. Annie's carotid doesn't exist, so we have to imagine. "I have a pulse!" I announce triumphantly, and Lucy grins.

The instructor nods. "Okay, I'm in a restaurant eating my dinner and you're sitting at the next table when suddenly . . ." She puts her hand up to her throat and makes choking noises.

"Your turn," Lucy says to me. "Go for it."

Suddenly I can't remember what to do. Then it comes to me. "Can you speak?" I ask.

The instructor shakes her head no and starts making a squeaking noise called stridor. She sounds like a seagull. I bend her forward, give four back blows, then put my arms around her and squeeze. "Christ! Not so hard!" she gasps between squeaks. I repeat the sequence and poke my finger in her mouth. She spits it out. "Hey! Am I conscious or what?" she asks angrily.

I remember I'm not supposed to do a finger probe if the victim is conscious. "Sorry," I say.

The instructor sighs. "You see a person with a deathlike appearance who's collapsed on the floor of the restaurant," she says.

I look at Lucy. "You do it."

"No," says the instructor, pointing at me. "I want you to do it."

Down on the floor I go again. I look up to see the other members of the class staring at me. I know they're waiting for me to say, "Are you okay?" I try to give a breath, but of course Annie's airway is supposed to be obstructed, and when I roll her over and slam her on the back she makes a hollow sound.

For a while I had a lover, someone I still think about and yearn for. I felt free when he and I were together, even though I had to sneak around like a criminal. "I've decided to stay over in the city because the driving is bad," I would tell my mother over the phone when the driving wasn't bad. I was taking an evening course at the university where he was studying, too.

"What's the matter with you?" Mother would ask. "And don't tell me nothing, because I know better."

If I hadn't told him I was falling in love with him, our affair might have lasted longer.

The night we said goodbye I stayed in the city because I couldn't stand the thought of going home to bed with Graham.

After we broke up I was depressed for weeks. I made an appointment to see my old therapist. "I don't love Graham anymore," I told her. But it was one thing telling her and another telling him.

He kept looking at me and saying, "You can't mean it."

I had chosen a time when Mother was visiting her sister in New Jersey. Graham had wanted to take me to the theater and then out for a late dinner. I discouraged him, saying I wasn't feeling well. I didn't want him spending a lot of money, only to have me blow everything to bits over cocktails at a fancy restaurant, or in the lobby during intermission.

"What are you doing?" the instructor asks. I've got Resusci-Junior facedown on my knees and I've just slapped his tiny back four times.

"Flip it over," Lucy whispers, and I want to kill her, because I know what to do next: I flip the baby over and press down with my fingers between its nipples. Then I'll try to give a breath, hoping for an airway.

The instructor sets the scene. "Still no airway," she says. "What next?"

This is getting ridiculous. In real life, the kid would have aspirated whatever it swallowed and died. Still, I have to keep trying. I look in his mouth. "I see something!"

"You don't see anything! Keep trying."

Something inside Junior has come loose. He rattles when I bang him on the back. Are real babies this flimsy?

Graham would have loved us to have children, but I wasn't sure how I felt about becoming a mother. I kept thinking about how hard it would be to raise a kid and care for an invalid at the same time. Of course, when we first married, my father was alive and it was impossible to predict that, within six months, we would become caregivers, but Graham never complained. His mother had died years before and I think he must have been very devoted to her. Like me, he is an only child. He and Mother get along famously. When Graham and I were having our difficulties he would try to get her to talk to me, which made matters even worse. At that time, I think all I really wanted was to be released from both of them.

Now Lucy is blowing into the baby's mouth, giving four quick puffs. I am halfway through my written exam. The others are standing in the hall, waiting for the instructor to sign their cards. Lucy puffs gently and the baby's chest rises just a little, the way it's supposed to. When I take Junior's pulse, his arm falls off. His little bowed legs lie, froglike, on the table. I go back to my test, which is harder than I anticipated. What is the ratio of breaths to compressions? I can't think anymore.

The instructor announces we have to come back tomorrow to get our cards because the secretary has left for the day and she doesn't know where the cards are kept.

"Well!" my mother exclaims when I walk in the door. "Here's our little Red Cross girl. Are you ready to save a life?" I look past her into the living room and there, just around the corner, I can see Graham's feet sticking out, crossed at the ankles. He is wearing the Nikes I gave him one Christmas in an effort to loosen him up. As I approach him he stands up and reaches out to touch me, then he quickly puts his hands in his pockets. He is wearing a new pair of jeans and a sweatshirt that looks too big. I've forgotten how much his hair has thinned. "I hope you don't mind that I asked him to stay for dinner," Mother says.

Then the strangest thing happens: I can't breathe. I run into my room and slam the door. They start yelling, "Are you all right?" and I think of my CPR class. If I don't answer, they'll issue a call for help. Suddenly I feel better, just knowing assistance is forthcoming.

When I open the door Graham is standing there, looking frantic. "I'm okay," I tell him. "You can come in." We sit down on the edge of our bed, and he leans toward me slightly, expectantly, poised between the need to stay and his instinct to go. I can hear my mother slamming things around in the kitchen. I can feel the tension in his body. When he touches me his skin is slightly moist, like a child getting ready to speak up in class.

"I need you," he says. "Do you think we could try living together again?"

I try to view him objectively. I try to see him through the eyes of another woman who might not notice that his skin is too white, his shoulders too rounded. But all I can feel is the emotional intensity he projects. His pale green eyes seem almost liquid, although I know he'd never cry. A tear shed in pleading for my affection would be too much to expect from Graham.

"What do I have to do to get you back?" he asks.

Lucy puts her Red Cross card in her wallet. "I guess this is goodbye," she says, smiling. Her pimply face is slightly flushed.

"Do you need a ride home?" I ask.

"My boyfriend is picking me up. Thanks anyway. And thanks for the moral support. I don't think I could have gotten through the course without you."

I watch her skip down the steps and run out to an old Toyota. The boy doesn't get out to open the door for her. She leans over and kisses him, then turns to wave at me.

Back in the classroom, the instructor is putting away the Annies. She has to peel off their chests and clean their parts. Heads and breathing tubes lie on the table, creating a perfect setting for Hawkeye and the gang from *M*A*S*H*. There is the scent of rubbing alcohol in the air. The instructor, intent on completing her job, empties the plastic air sacs and doesn't notice that I'm standing here, waiting to say goodbye. She is as busy as a nurse in intensive care.

Graham is waiting for me in the parking lot. As I walk to meet him, I wonder how and when I will be tested in real life. Will I see someone with a deathlike appearance on a beach or in a restaurant? Will I remember all the little details in sequence and, most important, will I be successful? Of course, I hope it never happens, but if it does, I want to be prepared.

THE VILLAGE

Although she's never been taken into custody before and can't know for sure what will happen next, Andrea Baxter-Smith assumes she won't be returning to her house by nightfall. If so, she wants to be prepared. She's packed a small suitcase with some essentials—a nightgown, a bathrobe, toiletries, slippers, and clean underwear for the next day. As she waits for the police, she tries to imagine the place where they will put her. Perhaps it will be drafty. In that case, she'll need the small throw, the blanket she keeps in the sitting room for use on chilly days. She smiles. It will be good to have something comfortable and familiar, she decides.

She unzips the cover of her suitcase and places the blanket inside, remembering the day she left the village in New Guinea. "We will miss you," the natives had said as they handed her the soft throw made from animal hairs and dyed ruby red with the tiny berries that grew everywhere. "Rituals of the Garden in a Primitive Society" was the title she'd chosen for her doctoral thesis, planning to subtitle it "The Supernatural in Theory and Practice." She'd been certain the paper would be greeted enthusiastically by her peers because so little was known about this particular tribe, and she'd believed she was the only Westerner to have been permitted to share its secret rituals.

At first she was frightened by what she saw, and shy about joining in the tribal rituals, but gradually, with the aid of hallucinogens supplied by the natives, her shyness disappeared and she became a believer.

She would have been content to stay in the village forever, but she needed to come back to New England for Carolyn's sake. She was not the kind of mother who could walk out on her daughter.

∞

"What are all those yucky stains under your fingernails?" Carolyn asked warily after Andrea, fresh off the plane from New Guinea, hugged her and told her how wonderful she looked. "Don't tell me you've been gardening with the natives."

"I have," Andrea replied with pride. "Anthropologists are supposed to dig around for facts, remember? Come here and give me a hug." Understandably eager to see her daughter, a senior at a women's college outside of Boston, yet mindful of the distance and what the fare would be, she'd splurged on a cab that took her straight to the dormitory. "What about coming to my hotel for the afternoon? I've got so much to tell you."

"I can't, Mom. I've got a class," Carolyn responded quickly.

"Afterward, then. I can pick you up for dinner," Andrea pushed, determined to break through the barrier Carolyn was imposing between them. In the time Andrea had been away, her husband, Sumner, had filed for divorce, prompted (she surmised) by her decision to pursue her studies and travel halfway around the world for purposes of research. Given the fact that Carolyn was living with her father, Andrea expected some resentment from the girl, but she also felt they had been close, too close to risk losing the special mother-daughter relationship they'd spent so many years cultivating.

"What'll you use for a car?"

"I planned to rent one to drive home. I'll just pick it up today instead of tomorrow," Andrea said. "Please, honey. I need to talk to you."

Carolyn hesitated. Then her face softened. "Oh, all right," she said. "Come at five-thirty. I'll meet you downstairs in the lounge." She took her mother's arm and gave it an almost affectionate squeeze. "Come on. I'll walk you to the corner, where you can get a cab."

Back at the hotel, Andrea made arrangements to rent a car, then ate a small lunch that seemed more like breakfast because her internal clock was still off-kilter. She tried to nap, but whenever she closed her eyes, she began to feel dizzy. Her mouth felt dry, also. She recognized the mild withdrawal symptoms she'd begun to suffer, symptoms connected with her investigative use of the hallucinogenic drugs. She wished she hadn't refused the villagers' offer of a going-away present, some more of the mildly addictive, dream-weaving substance she'd managed to hide in the lining of her suitcase, determined not to use it for fear of reestablishing a dependence.

Since she couldn't fall asleep, she decided to do some repacking. At the bottom of one suitcase was the throw. She pulled it out to admire its texture and color. It had an almost mesmeric effect. Before she realized what she was doing, she had kicked off her shoes and was stretching out on the bed. She covered herself with the throw, and almost as soon as she felt its softness envelop her body, she fell into a deep sleep.

When she awoke, the message light on her telephone was flashing and her travel alarm clock registered 6:45. A call to the desk revealed that Carolyn had been trying to reach her. "Honey, I'm so sorry," Andrea apologized. "You're probably starved. Listen, I can be on campus in a half hour."

"Didn't you hear the phone ringing?" Carolyn asked. "Oh, yeah. I forgot. Jet lag." She spat out the words angrily, making Andrea dread the thought of their dinner date.

Later, as they sat opposite each other in the pizzeria (Andrea had wanted to go someplace nicer, but Carolyn insisted she wasn't hungry enough for a fancy meal), Andrea could feel the mood lighten, perhaps because her hunger was being satisfied at last. She had awakened refreshed and famished. "I guess I was really exhausted from the long trip," she confessed. "Honey, aren't you going to eat that piece of pizza? God, I'm starved!"

"I told you, Mother. I'm not very hungry. I've been trying to cut down, anyway. Too much starchy college food, remember?"

"Mm," Andrea murmured, her mouth full. "I forgot how much I like junk food." When she finished her glass of wine, she tipped the carafe toward Carolyn's glass. "Want some more?" she asked. Carolyn shook her head. "No? Oh well, waste not, want not, I always say," Andrea giggled, filling her own glass to the brim.

Carolyn glared. "You're taking a cab, right? Or are you planning to cruise around in your rental car until you get nabbed for DWI? Gee, Mom, I hate to rush, but I've got to get to the library before it closes," she snapped.

Andrea signaled for the check. Why had she bothered to come here? she wondered. Carolyn's hostility made her wish she had stayed in New Guinea.

As they prepared to walk out into the chilly autumn night, Andrea thought there were times when Carolyn sounded just like Sumner—stuffy and prudish. She shuddered, thinking, *Two peas in a pod.*

The next day, Andrea drove back to New Hampshire and immediately noticed that everything looked barren in all the small towns she'd formerly considered picturesque. She'd become accustomed to the tropical lushness of the village. Why hadn't she planned to return to New England at peak foliage? Now the countryside was beginning to look bleak, and people were preparing for winter. On the car radio she heard commercials touting cold-weather service specials at local gas stations. As she drove through the endless small towns, she noticed store windows displaying warm outerwear and ice-fishing gear, and pedestrians walking briskly with their hands jammed in their pockets and their collars turned up to shield against the biting wind. She had to suppress the urge to turn the car around and head somewhere else, anywhere but Center Woods, where knotty problems refused to be easily solved. When she finally pulled into the driveway of their house, it was nearly one o'clock in the afternoon. Sumner would be at work until five. That left her plenty of time to gather the possessions she needed right away; she could send for the rest later.

As she opened the front door with the old-fashioned key she had used for so many years, she noticed the hallway had retained its musty odor. In the orderly living room, she detected a housekeeper's handiwork. The woman had even gotten the horrid crocheted antimacassars out of mothballs, and the overstuffed furniture they had inherited from Sumner's mother was heavily bedecked with string-like doilies, relics of another era.

She walked up the stairs slowly, almost shyly, feeling like a trespasser in the house she had called home for so many years, and stopped at the doorway to the master bedroom. Everything looked the same. Sumner had even left their wedding picture hanging on the wall above the bed. The chenille spread was stretched tightly across the pillows, a sure sign the cleaning woman had been there that morning, because Sumner had never been particular about making a bed.

She opened the door to Carolyn's room. It looked barer than the last time she had seen it. All the signs of high school mess had disappeared. Only the stuffed animals remained, souvenirs of an earlier time when every new boyfriend presented Carolyn with an addition to the menagerie. Andrea recalled the names of some of the gift-givers: Buzz, and Paul, and Joey, young studs who played football and were popular with the prettiest girls in the class. She wondered if there was a particular young man in Carolyn's life now. No mention had been made, but there had been little time for sharing intimacies. Perhaps it was just as well. She'd read that mothers and daughters reached a stage when they needed to grow apart. Besides, she herself enjoyed having certain secrets now that she was living on her own, and why should she deny Carolyn the same pleasure?

As she descended the stairs, she heard a familiar thumping noise that she identified immediately. They had always shut the cat in the cellar when no one was going to be home, and the cat would bump against the door when she heard someone enter the house, as if to say, *Let me out!* When Andrea opened the cellar door, Miss Kitty, a bushy-tailed calico, rushed past. The cat waited until Andrea filled her dish with kibble, then ate hungrily. When she finished, she licked her paws and looked up. "Miss Kitty," Andrea crooned. "Come here, baby." The cat backed away. Andrea knelt on the floor. "Darlin' girl, have you forgotten me?" she said as she reached out to touch her, but the cat ran back down the cellar stairs and remained there in an obstinate crouch. "Okay, if that's what you want," Andrea said as she closed the door, puzzled. She felt the animal was frightened, but of what?

"You'll be comfortable here, I think, Ms. Baxter-Smith," the innkeeper said, indicating a corner room at the rear of the second-floor corridor, which overlooked the garden. Andrea smiled, charmed. Even though the cleared patch of earth was gray and barren, she could imagine it in springtime filled with tender plants: vegetables and herbs to please the palate of diners who had read of the inn's famous cuisine and had traveled far to sample the culinary delights of New England. She admired the tasteful furnishings, which included a small desk she could use for her laptop. In the corner, an old-fashioned radiator hissed steam. The color scheme, dominated by rusts and golds, seemed earthy and comfortable. As she lifted her suitcases onto the bed, she realized it felt better being back in Center Woods than she'd anticipated. She decided there was no rush to look elsewhere for lodging. Of course, she would check with Sumner to make sure he didn't mind sharing the town with her.

Alone in the room, she unpacked, running her fingers over the bulge in the suitcase lining that marked the location of her one remaining cache of drugs. It would remain hidden, she decided, at least for the time being. Hadn't she had proved to herself that she could get along without it?

An hour later, she was typing so intently she failed to hear a knock on the door, and so it wasn't until early evening, when she left her room to go to supper, that she discovered a package lying in the hallway. As she unwrapped it, she recognized the particular nature and value of the contents: The villagers had sent her one of their most prized possessions, the cloak of a chieftain, a garment reserved for shamans. But *how*? There was no postage. It must have been hand-delivered, but by whom, and how had the bearer known where to find her?

In a recurring dream, she found herself back in the village participating in the sacred rites of the garden, sitting in the Circle of Mystery. When the moment approached for the supreme test of wills, it was she who was chosen by the shaman. She stood in the center and received the pile of rotting vegetables, proof that yet another curse had worked. She was frightened by the dream because she thought it meant the shaman was trying to transfer powers to her. The villagers believed a spell could be cast on the gardens cultivated by one's enemies, and the slightest provocation could invoke retribution. Uprooting vegetables was vindictive, but there were other, more terrible consequences that could result from exercising the powers. Andrea shuddered as she recalled one particularly gruesome episode involving a shaman's vengeance.

That evening, she made a number of inquiries in an attempt to uncover the identity of the messenger who had brought the gift. No one at the inn, in fact no one in all of Center Woods, had reported seeing a foreigner carrying an odd-shaped bundle through the streets of town. The delivery remained a mystery.

By springtime the divorce was final, and Andrea moved to a small rental property located on a quiet, familiar street at the edge of town, where she soon finished writing her dissertation and managed to convince Carolyn to join her during spring break. To Andrea's surprise, they enjoyed getting reacquainted in their new surroundings. Carolyn shared her plans to go to California after graduation, having convinced her father that studying computers on the West Coast was preferable to remaining outside of Boston unemployed.

In sum, Andrea was content. The house she rented was old but in good repair. It had a veranda and some gingerbread trim and a plethora of Victorian charm. Miss Kitty had come to live with her and was enjoying her newfound freedom, having to be shut in this cellar only on those days when Andrea traveled across the state to teach her freshman courses at the university, but continuing to keep her distance. The cat seemed to regard her as a threat and gave her the widest berth possible. This annoyed Andrea, who was not used to being rebuffed by animals and yearned to reinstate their former chummy relationship.

Since she used the front sitting room as her office, she decorated it with souvenirs of the village, giving the chieftain's cloak a place of honor on one wall, just above the landlord's vintage settee, where the off-white walls showcased its brilliance by day. On moonlit nights the fibers were shot with slivers of light, and Andrea could admire the silvery threads and glass beads that formed an intricate part of the fabric.

Although most of the residents of Center Woods adjusted to the new Andrea, her immediate neighbors, an older couple she had befriended when Carolyn was a youngster, remained aloof. Andrea tried not to let this bother her—having lived in New England most of her life, she was accustomed to Yankee reticence—but was surprised to find such coldness in people she had formerly regarded as friends. The week Carolyn visited she expected a thaw, figuring they'd want to see how their young protégée had fared. As an incentive, Andrea decided to invite them to dinner. Her telephone invitation, though coolly received, resulted in an acceptance, and Andrea remained hopeful.

When nobody showed, Carolyn blamed her. "You know how these people are," she said tearfully. "They hate anybody who's different. You're different. You went away and lived with weirdos, and now you've got strange stuff hanging on the walls. What did you expect them to do? They don't understand you." As if to reinforce her statement, she stormed upstairs to her room and slammed the door, causing the plaster around the frame to flake.

Curiously, it was about this time that Andrea and Sumner began to develop an easygoing relationship. It began the Saturday he invited her out to dinner at the inn. As they lingered over a bottle of Piesporter Riesling, his favorite wine, Sumner pleased Andrea by toasting the defense of her dissertation, which would occur later that month. In the spirit of the evening, Andrea silently pledged to forgive her unfriendly neighbors. She and Sumner drank to each other's happiness and to Carolyn's future on the West Coast. They decided that Carolyn should spend the summer with Andrea, and Andrea was pleased with the prospect of a lengthy visit with her daughter, though somewhat apprehensive, since they hadn't been getting along.

Soon the rift between the two women deepened. By mid-July they had begun to argue steadily, with Carolyn threatening daily to move to her father's house. Andrea felt a change of scene might be helpful, so they drove to Maine early one Saturday, in the middle of a heat wave, and found a vacancy in a small seaside motel. They spent the afternoon plunging their bodies into water so cold it numbed their skin.

Just as Andrea was beginning to relax, Carolyn announced she had changed her mind about going to California. "I'd rather wait a year," she said. "I'm tired of school. I need a break. I've applied for a waitressing job at the inn."

"How could you?" Andrea shouted, appalled. She knew Sumner had already paid Carolyn's tuition and board and wouldn't be able to get a refund. "You should have thought about this last spring, before your father plunked down that enormous sum of money!"

Carolyn jumped to her feet, scattering sand on the worn bedspread that had served them as a beach blanket for so many years. "I'm not the only one who does things on impulse," she huffed. "Look who went trotting off to New Guinea and left her family and everything! You can do whatever you want, but when it comes to Daddy and me . . ."

Bored by their own sultry mid-afternoon indolence, others began paying attention. "That's enough!" Andrea declared, reaching out to grab Carolyn's arm in a gesture of restraint. It had worked when the girl was five, but now served only to intensify the young woman's rebellion. Andrea felt her face redden. By now, Carolyn was halfway to the motel deck, so she gathered their things, pretending to be cool under the stares of nosy bystanders. *As if these women never fought with their daughters,* she thought angrily as she prepared to leave the beach. The sand was so hot it burned the soles of her feet. Her head began to pound. Suddenly she pictured the village and, for the first time in months, yearned to be there, immersed in its calm and simple way of life. She looked down at her hands and saw the purple shadows of stains that would never completely disappear and could almost smell the fragrant blossoms that had left their indelible stamp on her skin.

That night, Andrea was troubled by disturbing dreams. In an effort to restore tranquillity, she got out of bed. Taking care not to disturb Carolyn, she slid open the glass doors and stepped out onto the small balcony that overlooked the beach, which was deserted except for an old man with a metal detector who moved with the lumbering gait of a sleepwalker. The sand was lit gently by the lights in the motel parking lot, the stars, and a brilliant full moon. Andrea felt alone, yet not lonely, as if some protector hovered nearby. When she returned to bed, she knew she would sleep peacefully.

Carolyn was quiet during the trip back to Center Woods, and Andrea didn't press her for conversation. An uneven truce existed between them. Andrea had apologized for losing her temper, but she was still angry because the girl showed no signs of remorse.

When they arrived home, Carolyn removed her things from the car and went upstairs to her room while Andrea opened the cellar door to let out the cat, noting the animal wasn't in her usual place at the head of the stairs. "Carolyn, did you remember to put Miss Kitty in the cellar before we left?" she called.

"Yes. I even changed the water in her dish and made sure she had enough food."

"You sure she didn't get out?"

"Jesus Christ, Mother! Don't you believe anything I say? I put her in the cellar!"

"Hey, calm down. I just think it's odd that she isn't at the top of the stairs, where she always waits for us. Did you know the cellar lights are out? A fuse must have blown. Do me a favor. Get the flashlight I keep in the drawer of my bedside table, will you?"

There was a pause, and then Carolyn yelled, "The batteries are dead."

Andrea rummaged in the kitchen cabinet where she used to keep household necessities like spare batteries. "Damn. I'll have to get some in town," she muttered.

"What's this?" Carolyn asked, holding up a brown paper packet. "I found it in your night table drawer."

"Baking soda," Andrea said quickly. "I, uh, used it to clean my teeth when I was in the village."

Carolyn laughed. "Another use for Arm & Hammer, huh? You expect me to believe that? *Mom.* Just how gullible do you think I am? Whoa. Where'd you get this? Does Dad know?"

Andrea forced a smile. "It's not what you think it is," she said weakly. "The natives use it for medicinal purposes. Really, I don't know how it got in my suitcase. I must have shoved it in the drawer, not thinking." *Shit. How am I going to get out of this one?*

The telephone rang. "I'll get it," Andrea said, welcoming the interruption, but Carolyn had already picked up the receiver and was listening intently. "Yeah. Okay. I'll call you right back," she responded.

Still suffering from the strain of being interrogated, Andrea could feel her heart quicken with anticipation. "Who was that?" she managed to whisper, her mouth so dry she could hardly enunciate.

"Talk about weird! That was Mrs. What's-her-name from across the street, calling to say everyone's vegetables have been disappearing from their gardens. They think somebody's stealing them at night. She wants me to check ours and call her back."

Andrea shivered, then felt a strange sense of exhilaration as she watched Carolyn go out the back door and down to the garden. Seconds later she was running back toward the house, holding up some giant tomatoes. "Everything's fine!" she announced. "In fact, super. Do you know we've already got tomatoes and corn? You must really have picked up some pointers on gardening from those natives! We never used to have vegetables like these."

"Give me that woman's number and I'll call her," Andrea offered, trying to hide her excitement.

"No," Carolyn said. "I'll call. You go into town and get the groceries."

As Andrea backed the car out of the driveway, she knew exactly what would happen. Carolyn would wait until she was out of sight before opening the brown packet. *Arm &Hammer indeed.* Then she would suck the tip of her right index finger, press it into the white powdery substance, and lick it. *Mother, you're full of surprises.* The effects would be immediate: Within minutes she would convulse and fall to the floor. A few gasps of breath, and Carolyn would enter a state from which even the craftiest shaman failed to return.

It isn't that I don't love her, Andrea thought. *It's that I'm helpless to prevent this.*

An hour later, Andrea entered the house carrying two bags of groceries, put them on the hall table, and went down the cellar stairs. An overwhelming aroma of rotting vegetables hung in the air, along with another odor that she had trouble identifying, until she discovered the dead cat lying beneath a pile of overripe melons.

∞

When the police finish their investigation, they guide Andrea gently down the front steps. "What's that you're wearing?" the young rookie asks, pointing to the strange-looking garment she has draped over her shoulders.

"My mystical cloak," she whispers.

The two policemen look at each other and tap their foreheads knowingly. On either side of the street people are watching, hoping to catch a glimpse of their mysterious neighbor, who climbs into the backseat of the squad car as calmly as if she's going for an afternoon's drive.

"Wake me when we reach the village," Andrea says, and the two cops nod, thinking she means the middle of town.